Tails of Ugly Creek

by

Cheryel Hutton

Ugly Creek Series, Book 4

Tails of Ugly Creek

Cover Art by *Debbie Taylor*

The Wild Rose Press, Inc.
PO Box 708
Adams Basin, NY 14410-0708
Visit us at www.thewildrosepress.com

Publishing History
First Fantasy Rose Edition, 2018
Print ISBN 978-1-5092-2163-9
Digital ISBN 978-1-5092-2164-6

Ugly Creek Series, Book 4
Published in the United States of America

I forced back the strong desire to laugh. Poor Hunter had a faery treed and didn't know what to do with her. Didn't even realize what she was. What was I going to do? I recognized what she was, but not anything about her kind. I did know at least some faeries spoke English. "Hello." I tried to keep my voice quiet and friendly.

She looked at me and blinked, let out another soft, musical sound, then took off out the bedroom door and down the steps. A shimmer followed her, and for a moment it looked like glitter hung in the air. Hunter rushed after her, probably trying to see where she was going. Personally, I was just relieved she hadn't flown out the window.

He turned and looked at me, his expression the textbook version of confused. I smiled in spite of myself. "We got sneaked up on."

"Boy, that's the truth. Good thing she wasn't armed and dangerous."

"Not much dangerous around here, really. Mostly just odd and unexpected."

He glanced toward the door. "I'm beginning to see that."

Dedication

To the women of Chattanooga Area Romance Authors:
Kelle Z. Riley, Nita Wick, Leigh Riker, Laurie White,
and Carrie Nichols. I miss you all so much.

~*~

CARA rocks!

Chapter One

The marauders fell upon us...

Okay, it was a pack of teenagers. Wild, loud, disruptive teenagers grouped together by the desire to irritate adults as much as possible without getting in trouble. From what I overheard, these were advanced-level high school students who had been sent to the public library as a learning experience. Their task was to find books for reports. So began the invasion of the normally quiet Ugly Creek Library, bringing hope to the librarians that these kids would see the importance of libraries, and annoyance to the regular patrons.

I was, of course, there to write. I was at my regular, excellent table near a window. I'd worked for hours at home, but my characters were still talking to me, so I'd taken my trusty laptop to this magical place devoted to books. Things were going well until the invasion. I like teenagers generally, act like one quite often, but this was my career. I'm a novelist with a rapidly approaching deadline, so I take *scriptum interruptus* seriously.

It's hard to break my concentration, I write to loud music, after all, but this pack was determined. In an effort to not allow frustration to screw up the flow I'd enjoyed all morning, I took my laptop and headed toward the back where I happened to know there was one tiny table. It wasn't a lot quieter back there, but it

1

was better, and I'd take what I could get. I was on a roll, and I wanted to keep rolling. And no, I didn't bring my headphones. I don't normally use them at the library. I write to classic rock music at home, so changing to a relatively quiet environment frequently stimulates my muse.

It only took a couple of minutes to get back into the fictional world.

"Mind if I sit here?"

I looked up, and standing in front of me was a tall guy wearing a bow tie. A bow tie. What the flea-bite-heck kind of dude under fifty wears a bow tie? Then again, at least he was closer to my age than to the yapping hoard of hormone charged irritants. "Sure."

"Thanks," he said, as he maneuvered extra-long legs so he could sit. "You seem to have the only relatively quiet table in this place."

"Yes, I do."

There was peace for a moment, then a hand came across the table. "I'm Hunter. Hunter Devereux, and I'm really sorry to have invaded your working spot."

I looked up, ready to tell him to either shut up or go play with the kiddies. But then I saw the most amazing pair of hazel eyes. My brain went on hold, and my hand moved toward him. "Terri Quinn."

He had awesome thick hair. Seriously dark brown that bordered on black, the strands glossy and cut to just brush his collar.

"Where do I know that name from?"

I smiled and tried to look properly modest. "I've made the *New York Times* list a couple of times. Well, four, actually."

"Wow! Congratulations. Fiction or non?"

I smiled. He was not bad looking, even if he did invade my territory. "Fiction. Women's Fiction, to be specific."

"Oh." He busied himself with opening his laptop.

Irritation ran laps in my stomach. He'd *so* better not be going where I thought he was. "*Oh?*"

He kept his gaze on his computer as he shrugged.

I leaned toward the bow tie wearing snob. "Let me guess, only literary works deserve to be on a bestselling list."

"Absolutely not. Commercial fiction can definitely be list-worthy."

Hot coals burned in my veins. "But not women's fiction?"

"Look obviously you're an excellent writer, and I don't know what your books are like, but the vast majority of women's fiction is lightweight. It is simply women talking about their lives. But better than romance, of course."

I leaned forward, the better to smell his anxiety. "Would you like to tell me what's wrong with romance fiction?"

He straightened his back, and I waited for him to make a cow turd of himself.

"Romance," he said, "tends to be formulaic and predictable. The genre also suggests that women are nothing if not connected romantically to a man.

My hands clenched, as fire filled my veins. The growl deep in my throat was out before I realized it was coming. Hunter's eyes widened, and I smiled. "Just how many romance novels did you read before coming to that conclusion?"

He made a dismissive little noise. "Why would I

waste my time reading romance?"

I stood so fast my chair tipped over backwards and hit the floor with a loud thunk. I put my palms on the table and leaned so close, his pupils dilated. "You are an arrogant hair on the butt of a flea."

"Hairs can't be arrogant."

"Oh, get over yourself." I picked up the fallen chair and planted my derriere back in the seat. No way was I letting this overgrown spoiled child bully me into leaving. This was my library and my table. I looked down at my laptop screen, put my fingers on the appropriate keys, and started typing in spite of the fact that I had no idea where the scene was going. Or what I was typing, for that matter. I felt Hunter's gaze on me as I finally managed to pick up the thread of my manuscript. I ignored his idiotic self and kept on putting words on the page.

"I'm sorry, I need to learn to keep my big mouth shut. I teach English and American Literature as well as creative writing, so I'm used to being verbal about my opinions."

I looked over my computer screen to meet his gaze. "You teach *creative writing*?"

"Yes, at Laurence Talbot College."

"Your poor students."

He winced. "I guess I deserved that."

"I mean it. Teachers like you can damage a student enough to prevent them from ever trying what they're hardwired to do. Stories for and about women are just as important as those for and about men."

"It's not about gender, I just try to point students toward emulating quality writing."

I respected the library too much to deck him right

4

there. I'd catch him later and show him how female genre writers fight. "You need to quit before I do something you'll regret."

He blew out a breath. "I insulted you, I know—"

"And my cousin, the contemporary romance writer."

"And your cousin."

He wasn't sounding nearly contrite enough, so I let some of my predatory instinct show through. "And every women-centered genre writer in the world."

He opened his mouth, looked into my eyes, and his expression shifted. Maybe it was a sliver of understanding, or a subconscious reaction to my desire to chew his leg off. Either way, he sounded serious when he repeated, "And every women-centered genre writer in the world."

Satisfied, for the moment anyway, I turned back to my manuscript.

"I really am sorry. This research is driving me crazy."

I looked at the stack of books beside his laptop. They all involved local history. "Why are you researching Ugly Creek?"

"I saw a documentary about this area and was intrigued. I started digging, and decided it would be a great subject for a book."

So he thinks he can write, huh? I glanced toward the stack beside his computer again, then met his gaze. "Like that's never been done before."

"I'm hoping to put a new spin on the subject."

"Of course."

He looked at his watch. "I have a phone call I need to make." He stood and gathered up his things. "Later."

I gave a little nod. He left and I turned back to my own work. I was surprised at how hard it was to push my irritation with this Hunter person out of my mind long enough to finish the next scene. He was handsome, his voice was deep and sexy, and there was something about him that intrigued me.

Too bad he was a pain in the butt.

****

It should have been a perfect afternoon. My writing work had been smooth and fun. It was early fall in Tennessee, the perfect place to enjoy the season. I sat on the couch in my Aunt Ruth's house, watching the sun dip behind the mountains. The light reflecting off the autumn leaves cast brilliant shades of gold and red and yellow and orange, creating a beautiful landscape just begging to be admired and enjoyed.

Unfortunately, I was in no mood for gorgeous colors. This was release week for my latest book, and when my phone rang I was expecting good news. I was wrong.

My heart dropped and bounced off my stomach. "What do you mean, I'm not on the list?"

"I'm sorry," my agent said. "I know this is upsetting, Terri, but very few authors make the *New York Times* Bestseller List even once in their careers. Making it with every single book would be a miracle." Hannah's usually comforting voice wasn't. Not today.

"It's release week, if not this week, then never."

"Sometimes it just happens, Terri."

I wanted to scream, but it wasn't my agent's fault my latest book wasn't happily climbing the *New York Times* bestseller list like a good little women's fiction. "What did I do wrong?"

6

"Nothing I saw. You know publishing is a crazy business, especially when you factor in the always shifting propensities of the reading public."

"Bull baloney. Something didn't work. Something in *Sisters, Sand, and Secrets* wasn't as good as the four books before it."

"Actually," I heard the reluctance in her voice, "Your sales were down for *Sand and Margaritas*, just not as significantly as for *Sisters, Sand and Secrets*."

I swallowed. "You're saying the 'Beach' series isn't working."

"It's working, just not the way it did at the beginning."

My heart beat so hard I could feel it in my throat. "My publisher isn't going to drop me, are they?"

"No, but I doubt I can get the same terms for your next contract."

Less advance, fewer perks, big sense of failure. "What can I do, Hannah?"

"You're a fast writer. You could look at a different direction, maybe even with a different name."

For a moment I couldn't breathe. "You mean starting all over again."

"Not if you get in front of this. Maybe try a different genre and let me get it out there before your next 'Beach' book comes out."

Tears burned my eyes, and I fought hard not to fall apart.

"Look," Hannah's gentle voice reached out almost like she was physically touching me. "How about you think about what you'd be willing to do, and I'll get in touch with your editor and see if we can figure something out."

We ended the call, and I leaned back with a big, deep, pathetic breath. I had to think. No it wasn't the end of the world, but it was a big blow. I didn't intend to go down without a fight. I just had to figure out a plan.

Scrappy, my white and yellow ball of kitty fur, leaped onto the couch then climbed into my arms. She snuggled against my belly and proceeded to purr. As upset as I was, it was impossible to not smile at the little creature.

Even with Scrappy's comforting warmth and sweet purr, it didn't take long for me to realize I couldn't think sitting and staring at the wall, so I got up and headed toward the kitchen. Near the back door, I put Scrappy down on the floor, slid out of my clothes, and allowed my body the freedom to alter. Thirty seconds or so later, I burst through the doggie door as a collie. Scrappy, familiar with the procedure, had gone on through the door and was waiting for me outside.

Racing around the house and back and forth across the yard, relaxation loosened the tension in my body. The best thing about being a shifter is having the ability to run full-tilt on four paws on soft grass with the wind in my face. There is nothing better in the world!

As I came around the house, I noticed our neighbor Miz Carlisle, AKA Miz Pain-In-The-Butt glaring hard at me. Figuring irritating her would be a decent way to kick all the worrying out of my system, I headed toward the white picket fence. Yes, really. It might be cliché, but the neat white lines are a beautiful finishing touch on my aunt's home. A few bits of hedge and Miz Pain's flower garden completed the divider between the yards.

"Go home, you smelly beast!" my neighbor yelled.

Since I couldn't speak English in this form, I did not point out that not only did I have a lovely canine smell that other dogs frequently complimented me on, but also that I was, in fact, on my side of the fence, and thus at my current place of residence. Instead, I answered in my most adorable bark.

"Stop that horrid barking, you mangy mutt. You'll scare my Bumpkins."

I wasn't a mutt, or mangy, and that... Wait a minute, where was that spawn of Satan? I spun just as the feline scent reached me.

The cat was a beautiful black with white paws, chest, and nose-mouth area. You'd never know by looking at him that he wasn't a sweet, friendly cat. But he lived to torment dogs. His paw raked at my face, and I barely missed a scratched nose. I backed up, and he followed. I could see by the look in his eyes he was hoping for another shot at me.

I growled, and he smiled. The furry terrorist knew I'd never hurt him. He swiped at me again, and I reached out and pushed at his shoulder. I barely touched him, but he reacted with that high-pitched yowl only cats can manage. Streaking through the fence boards, he was beside his human slave in seconds. She scooped him up, giving me a scowl that would probably freeze me solid if she kept it up long enough.

"Good boy," she told the demon cat. "You keep that nasty creature on its side of the fence. It wouldn't do for it to dig around in my flowers, would it? No it wouldn't." She headed toward the house, babbling about her flower bed.

The woman was obsessed with her stupid flowers. As she walked across her yard, she kept glancing back toward me, as if she thought I was planning something.

I considered hopping over and digging in her precious New England Asters, but that would be mean. Right?

A red car pulled into our driveway, and I headed toward the house. I couldn't wait to hear about my cute, red-headed cousin's latest romantic adventures with her handsome boyfriend, Ace. I was still pulling my clothes back on when Shay strolled into the kitchen, grabbed a bottle of water from the fridge, took a long drink, then leaned back against the counter. Her smile was wide, her expression relaxed.

"You look like one seriously satisfied woman."

She didn't even glance my way, just smiled wider. "What can I say, Ace is a talented man."

"Well, that's an interesting statement."

And the smile got even wider. Any more and her face would tear.

I grabbed her in a quick hug. "I'm happy for you, Shay." And I was. Maybe a little jealous too, but that didn't mean I wasn't glad she finally caught a break. My sweet cousin's life hadn't been easy.

"Thanks." She grinned. "You're next."

"If you say so."

"I do." She turned and headed toward her bedroom. "I have to pack. I'm spending a few days in Kentucky with Ace."

It took a second for my brain to process what she'd said. "Kentucky? With Ace?"

"Yep, there's an animal rescue near where his parents live. The rescue is having an adoption fair, and he asked me to come along."

A smug smile pulled at my face. "He's taking you

to meet his parents. That's awesome."

"Don't say that yet. They might hate me." She turned toward her bedroom.

"They won't. Hey, what about your new manuscript? Didn't you say your agent wanted you to get it to her by the end of the month?"

"I'll take my laptop. I'm almost finished anyway. It'll be fine."

I shook my head as I watched her walk away. I be willing to bet money that she'd come home smiling, and with a non-existent word count. I wasn't jealous. Really, I wasn't.

Okay, I lie to myself sometimes.

Chapter Two

Two days later, I was back at the Ugly Creek Library. This time it was for exactly the opposite reason as before. I wasn't shooting out words like a slot machine jackpot, I was pulling words from my muse one letter about every twenty minutes. In other words, I was in big do-do.

I glared at my laptop screen as if it was responsible for my inability to type words on it, but it was me I was kicking in the rump. Whatever was wrong with my latest books was my own doing. Not that I had any freaking idea what the problem was. Earlier that morning, I'd spent almost two hours on the phone with my agent going over possibilities, and I still didn't have a clue. As promised, she'd spoken with my editor, and we discussed everything either of them could come up with. I had a list of things to try with the new manuscript, but nobody was sure if those changes would solve the problem, or make the situation worse. So there I was, glaring at my screen and wondering if I was about to go belly-up in the literary world.

"Excuse me," the familiar male voice said.

I looked up into those gorgeous hazel eyes. "Hunter."

"Sorry to disturb you again." He held a small notebook with a ribbon wrapped around it, and a bow right in the middle. "I wanted to apologize for yesterday. For invading your space and insulting you."

I reached for the ribbon-wrapped apology. "Thank you."

"I hope this is okay." He shrugged. "I've never met a writer who doesn't like notebooks."

"I like them, that's for sure." I slipped the ribbon off and opened the six-inch, hardback, blank, pink notebook. Little silver stars were scattered across the front, and inside the pages had snippets of star trivia printed at the bottom. "This is adorable. Thank you."

"I'm glad you like it." He gently touched my shoulder. "I'll get out of your hair now."

"You don't have to do that."

He eyed me curiously. "Are you sure you want me and my big mouth at your table?"

"Sure. Why not?"

"Hey, if you can't think of a good reason, then I'm not going to help you." He took his laptop case around to the other side of the table and sat in the chair opposite me.

I tried to get into my story, but I just couldn't concentrate. What was so different from all my other books? Was I just plain losing my writing mojo? Would I have to find a different way to keep myself up in the way I'd become happily accustomed?

Would I fail at the one thing I was good at?

I looked across the table. Hunter was a teacher. He didn't know me. He'd never read my stuff. He didn't even like women's fiction. He clearly spoke his mind about literary projects. He could probably tell me the hellacious honeydew melon what was wrong with the story I was struggling to force out.

I mentally rolled my eyes. He'd probably hate

everything about my stuff. He would have his mind made up before he even started. What good would it do to ask the advice of a person like him? The part of my brain with the logic generator answered the question. Because he would have a unique perspective. Because he was trained to know what was wrong.

What did I have to lose? The part of my brain that was solely me answered: my pride.

Okay, what was a little pride damage compared to losing my career? But would he even be willing to "waste" his time reading one of my books? Would he hate it so much he'd tell me it was horrible and needed to be shredded and scattered over the nearest landfill? Would he find the problem, save my career, and humiliate me?

"Are you all right over there?"

I looked up at him. "What?"

He frowned. "Your face was scrunched up like you were trying to type with your mind, which was sort of amusing. Then you went pale and your hand is trembling so I thought I'd better make sure you're all right."

I closed my eyes and leaned back in my seat. Well, this was humiliating. "I'm worried."

"Would it help to talk about it?"

I looked at Hunter, and saw concern. Maybe he had mastered the expression so that he could use it with his students, but right now, it seemed a good idea to assume it was real and see how he reacted to my problem. I leaned toward him. "My last two titles haven't sold as well as the ones before them."

"Define 'as well.' Do you mean a few hundred or thousands?"

I forced myself to look him straight in the eye. "I didn't hit the NYT list with the last book."

I don't know what I expected, but what happened was his eyebrows pulled together and his mouth opened. "Oh, Terri. I'm so sorry."

I shrugged, but it was a pathetic movement. "Could you…would you mind…" Oh great, now I was being a scared baby. The worst that could happen was he'd say no.

I raised my chin, met his gaze again, and made my mouth ask the question. "Would you look at the last book and tell me what you think the problem might be?"

"I'd be honored."

"Honored?"

He took a deep breath. "Terri, I may be a big-mouthed, opinionated jerk, but you are a bestselling author. For you to ask me to look at your work is an honor."

I tried to make the words light and teasing. "Even if it is women's fiction?"

He winced. "I honestly believe literary fiction is the filet mignon of the writing world. On the other hand, I love hamburgers too. Commercial genre fiction is the workhorse. Literary is something you have on special occasions." He touched my hand. "I'll be kind to your work, I promise."

"Not too kind." I managed a weak smile. "I want to know what's wrong with the damn thing."

"How many of your novels have been bestsellers?"

"Five. I sold more of each of my first three releases, then four through seven were solid hits. The eighth hit low, and the ninth didn't hit at all." I tapped the top of the laptop screen. "This is number ten."

"So it would be best if I read both the seventh and the ninth, so I could compare what worked and what apparently didn't."

I shrugged. "I have copies at home. You can have all of them if you want."

He smiled. "I'll start with the seventh and ninth, then we'll go from there."

"Thank you."

"You're welcome, but I do have a favor to ask in return."

I managed to hold the groan inside. Little voices saying things about making a deal with the devil swirled in my head. "What kind of favor?"

"I need somebody to show me around town, help me find the places I want to go, and suggest other places or people or things to check out."

I studied his expression for a time, until he wiggled in his seat nervously, assessing his sincerity. When I was satisfied I leaned back and crossed my arms over my chest. "I would be happy to be your guide, but you have to tell me more about what you're doing, what you intend to accomplish."

"Fair enough."

I smiled. "I'll bring you the books tomorrow."

"Sounds good. Meet me at Ugly Creek tomorrow morning at nine."

A smile pulled at my lips. "You mean the tiny picnic area at the actual creek?"

"That's the place." He held out his hand. "Deal?"

I gripped his hand firmly as I smiled. "Deal. This should be fun."

"From your lips to God's ears."

I went back to my manuscript wondering what I'd just gotten myself into.

****

Everybody loved Blackwood Antiques, but I doubt that many loved it for the same reason I did: all those wonderful scents. From what I've heard, most humans don't really like the smells that old things give off. At the very least, they dislike dust and the smell of long-ago molded fabric. Me, I love it. I wandered around the shop, trying to be inconspicuous with my sniffing.

"Good afternoon, Terri. How are things?"

I smiled at the short, curly-haired woman who had just stepped out of the back area of the store. Then I caught the scent of recent sickness and saw her pale face. "Are you okay, Stephie?"

She gave a casual shrug. "Fine, just got hold of something that didn't agree with me."

A door opened upstairs and a beautiful, big boy with both Lab and German shepherd heritage loped down the stairs.

"Hello, Dingo," I said.

He rushed over to me with a big grin and a seriously wagging tail. I gave him a good head scratching and told him how he was the best doggie in the entire world, and he lapped up the attention like nectar. Out of the corner of my eye, I caught a glimpse of Stephie slipping into the back of the store. A moment later Dingo and I heard her throwing up.

We looked into each other's eyes. "Your human isn't feeling well," I said.

He whined a little, letting me know he was concerned.

I gave him a little smile. "I think she's going to be

fine." I leaned closer to him. "You might have to learn to share some of that attention you're convinced you can't live without." Footsteps from the stairs pulled my attention from the dog, and I smiled at the man who'd just reached the bottom. "Hi, Jake."

"I see Dingo already conned you into giving him attention."

"I don't mind. He's a nice dog, aren't you, boy?"

"He's a big baby, that's what he is." Jake was looking around, and I could smell the concern.

"Your wife is in the bathroom, I believe. I don't think she's feeling very well."

He frowned. "I think she needs to see a doctor."

The sound of a door opening had him on his feet and headed for the back. I played with Dingo, and tried to ignore the conversation, but ears can't be closed so I caught the back and forth about doctors, lying down, and when to tell people the news.

I smiled into Dingo's fur. Sometimes it was fun to be part canine. You never know when you might discover something that makes all the bad just fly away.

Chapter Three

The next morning was damp and chilly. Rain overnight had dampened everything while lowering the temperature. A gust of wind made me shiver, and I wondered how long it would be before it actually started freezing and snowing and such. I'll admit to being used to warm, sunny Florida, but this was ridiculous.

I heard him coming, but I didn't turn until I felt a hand on my shoulder.

"You're shivering," Hunter said.

"Just a little. I think somebody flipped the 'on' switch for fall a little too soon."

"It's probably nice and warm in Jacksonville right now."

I narrowed my eyes at him. "You've been researching me."

"Just a little Internet searching." He wrapped his warm jacket around my shoulders, and heat that had nothing to do with insulating material, fired in me.

"Thank you," I managed.

He only grinned as he put his arm around my shoulders and we walked together down the embankment to the edge of the little stream.

"This creek is anything but ugly," he said. "How in the world did they come up with a name so opposite reality?"

"I have no idea. I've wondered that myself."

His scent rose from his jacket and surrounded me. I liked that a little too much.

"You didn't try to find out?"

"It's hard to get straight answers around here."

"Tell me about it." He picked up a stone and tossed it into the creek. "Half the time all you can find is a supernatural explanation, not the real one."

What if the supernatural explanation *is* the real one? I looked off into the distance. I couldn't tell him anything. Nothing. He might smell fantastic, but he was a stranger. Ugly Creek's secrets had to stay secret.

A movement caught my attention. I saw a furry leg barely visible from behind a tree. "There are things scientists can't put into little boxes."

"Yet, but there are some things that just can't possibly be real."

"If you say so."

"Science says so."

I heard voices behind us, and looked back to see a couple and two young children at the concrete picnic table. I smiled, thinking how great it would be to have kids. "What kind of things would you classify as impossible?"

Hunter shrugged. "Vampires, werewolves, men from Mars, faeries, leprechauns, should I go on?"

"Bigfoot!" the child's voice rang through the clearing, startling me.

I turned to see the little boy, who looked to be about first grade size, come tearing down the embankment toward the water. A man, possibly his dad, came running after the kid, but caught his foot in a fallen tree limb, and stumbled. It only took him seconds to get his balance back, but by then the boy was splashing into the water.

I dropped Hunter's jacket and started toward the kid, but Hunter had already reached him.

"Whoa there, cowboy. Where're you heading?"

"I want to see Bigfoot," the boy said, as he continued splashing through the water.

Hunter lunged, and his long legs gave him enough advantage to grasp the kid's arm. "There's no such thing as Bigfoot."

The boy pulled against Hunter in earnest, shoving against him with his free hand. "Yes, there is Bigfoot. Ask my daddy!"

Hunter pulled the child, arms and legs flailing, toward the shore. "I know it's awesome to think there are Bigfoot, but there aren't."

Abruptly the boy broke into loud, wailing sobs. "You're lying!"

The father reached them, and Hunter released the boy.

"Tell him, Daddy," the kid sobbed into his dad's shoulder.

"Let's get you home and into dry clothes."

"Why don't you tell him the truth?" Hunter stood midstream, arms crossed across his chest and glaring toward the other man. "He could have gotten hurt chasing a figment of somebody's imagination."

"Why's he being mean, Daddy?"

The man stopped and looked at Hunter. "Thank you for helping take care of Sebastian, I do appreciate it. But you need to mind your own business."

Back at the shore, the man headed toward their car while the woman gathered the little girl into her arms and followed after him. She shot a hard glare at Hunter before she turned to put the child in her car-seat. He slogged back through the water to where I stood.

I'd already rescued his jacket from where I'd dropped it, and I wrapped it around his shoulders. "You're shivering."

"Water is cold," he said through chattering teeth.

"Are you staying at Rosemary's Bed and Breakfast?"

"Only place in town."

"True." I opened the passenger door of my car. "I'll take you so you can dry off and change."

"I'll get your car wet," he protested, as he slid into the seat.

I started the car and turned the heater on high. "No big deal. It wouldn't be the first time."

He gave me a look and I worked to rein in my giggle. "I have a dog. A collie."

"Dogs are great. What's his name?"

"*Her* name is Trixie, and she's a very special dog."

"You'll have to introduce us sometime."

"I'll do that." I swallowed the laugh and focused on pulling the car into the tiny parking lot of the Bed and Breakfast.

We walked together into the building, where he headed toward the stairs and I found a seat in the lobby. The rustic look of the room was meant to be calming, but it made me want to shift and run around outside. I have to admit, the thought of Hunter upstairs, taking off his wet jeans, had me thinking things that weren't appropriate toward an arrogant, opinionated man like him.

I picked up the first magazine I saw and flipped

through it. I tried to focus my mind on the beautiful homes in *Southern Living*, but my mind was swirling. I tossed the magazine back onto the table just about the time the door opened and Mr. McDuffy walked in.

Okay, I'll admit I've never met Mr. McDuffy, or as everybody called him, Duffy, but I'd heard enough stories not to recognize him. The man is not quite four feet tall, has bright red hair, and is rumored to have a stash of gold at his house. Not that anybody had a clue where that house might be. Aunt Ruth says he's a leprechaun, and I had no trouble believing it.

Whatever he was, he walked over to the check-in desk and rang the little bell. "Top o' ye mornin', doll."

A middle-aged woman wearing a soft blue dress that suited her warm brown hair, came out a doorway. "Duffy, what are you doing here?"

He leaned his hip against the big mahogany desk. "Ya know why I'm here, Rosemary."

She sighed as she shook her head. "You never give up, do you?"

"Never. We're destined ter be together."

A noise drew my attention from the drama playing out in front of me. And I saw Hunter pause on his way down the stairs and stare at the couple at the desk. He shook his head like he was trying to shake away what he had just seen, then picked up the pace the rest of the trip down and over to me.

I bit back the smile as we walked out to my Fiat and waited until we were on our way to ask, "So you've never seen a leprechaun before?"

He snorted. "There's no such thing as a leprechaun."

Amusement rose in my chest, but I ignored it.

"Sure about that?"

He turned his smug expression on me. "Positive."

"So you're sure you would know a leprechaun if you saw one? What would you say they look like?"

He frowned. "You seriously want me to describe a mythical creature?"

"Humor me."

"Okay, a little guy. Maybe three feet tall, Santa belly, bright red hair and beard. He's evil, or at least not very nice. Has a pot of gold somewhere. How's that?"

"If I told you McDuffy is a—"

"Don't go there, Quinn."

The laughter was getting harder to hold back. "Fine. But remember this conversation for later."

As soon as we parked, Hunter slid out of my car and over to his. I thought maybe he had decided to run away, but he was only going for a camera. I watched as he snapped shots of the copper sign with historical details of the creek. He also shot pics of the picnic tables and went down the embankment again. I stood back as he took pictures of the creek area. I figured I'd stay out of his way, maybe guard against invaders—human, Bigfoot, or otherwise.

He headed back my way, smiling as he approached. "Afraid of the Bigfoot?"

"Nope. I was afraid this time I'd wind up in that freezing water."

"You've got a point. It was cold for me. Your thin Florida blood couldn't handle it."

"Where is your thicker blood from?"

He narrowed his eyes. "So you didn't search me on the Net? I think I'm insulted."

I playfully slapped at his arm, and he laughed.

"Okay, I was born in Memphis."

"Tennessee or Arkansas?"

"Smart girl. Tennessee." His voice had dropped an octave.

"Southern boy," I whispered.

"And proud of it."

"Where to now?"

He brushed a stray strand of hair out of my face, and his touch sent warm tingles through me. "I was thinking maybe I could take you to lunch and you could give me some guidance about the best places to gather information and local color."

I shrugged. "I'll do my best."

Thirty minutes later we were sitting at a table on the Taco King porch finishing our plates of delicious tacos. The mid-October breeze was a little chilly, but the bright sunshine warmed the air, making eating outside a pleasant, relaxing experience.

"Do you have any suggestions for places to go for research?"

"You mentioned a different take on Ugly Creek history. If I knew what that was, it would help me figure out which places to suggest."

"Fair enough. I'm planning to look deeper into some of the most prevalent stories and debunk the paranormal aspects."

Thankfully I managed to swallow the sip of cola I'd just taken. "Debunk?" I choked out.

"Yes." Hunter's grin had a smug twist. "Do you have a problem with that?"

"Why?" It was all I could think to say.

He shrugged. "Because nobody else has, and the truth needs to be told."

I considered my options. "You do realize the people here take their local stories very seriously?"

"Including creatures and events that can't possibly be true. That's what you're saying, right?"

"Creatures and events that you believe can't be true. Yes."

His expression was downright pity-filled. "Please tell me you don't buy in to that crazy Bigfoot stuff."

I swallowed what I wanted to say and stuck with, "What I do or don't believe isn't your problem. It's what the community believes."

"I've thought about that. I'm not sure it's a matter of belief as much as a matter of money."

I shook my head in an unsuccessful attempt to understand. "Say what?"

He leaned toward me. "Tourism. The locals want to keep their mystique so as to attract tourists."

"Hunter, Rosemary's B&B is the only place in town to spend the night. Not very conducive to your alleged tourist trade."

"Maybe they don't want to encourage a night life. Doesn't matter anyway. Whatever the reasons are, I'm not aiming for tourists. I'm writing for people who are interested in history. Real history, not tall tales or legends." He leaned forward as he put his hand over mine. "Will you help me, Terri?"

What else could I do? "Sure. Just let me figure out the best places for you to visit."

"Fair enough. What do you think about the train museum this afternoon? I saw a brochure and it looks very interesting."

"It's a fascinating place steeped in history. Plus, I've heard rumors that aliens sometimes hang out in the woods near there."

"Then that's where we'll go." He gave my hand a firm, but gentle, squeeze, along with a big smile that had me grinning back like one of those silly designer dogs.

He paid for lunch, and we headed out. I left my windows down on the drive to the museum, hoping the fresh air would clear my head.

****

I parked in the museum lot and got my things. "I totally forgot to give these to you earlier." My hand shook a little as I handed copies of my books to Hunter. As he took them from me, his fingers brushed mine and warm tingles moved up my arm from the point of his touch.

"I thought maybe you'd changed your mind about letting an opinionated professor like me look at your work," he said.

"I am a little leery," I admitted.

He leaned in so close his lips brushed my ear. "I promise I'll be gentle."

I gasped, and the spicy, musky, totally male scent of Hunter Devereux all but knocked me off my feet. Who knew a human male could affect a woman like that?

"Are you all right?"

"Huh?" I looked into his grinning face, and the enchantment ended. My face went abruptly hot, and I wanted to race away into the woods. What the hell was wrong with me?

"Let me put these in my car, then I need to get to work."

I managed a nod, and as he turned to open the door

of his car, I rushed off toward the museum.

Outside the main building, sitting on a section of track that dated from the Civil War, was a huge steam engine. I decided the black hunk of hard metal was probably the inspiration for the huge, deadly robots that populated many science fiction books and movies. It wouldn't take much imagination at all to transform the bulk into a moving thing of death and destruction.

"She's gorgeous," Hunter's voice said from beside me.

I looked at him, wondering what he'd seen. Oddly, he was looking right at the big engine. I looked at the hulking piece of intimidation again, and saw the same thing I'd seen before. "Deadly robots."

"Excuse me?" His lips twitched.

"Did I say deadly robots out loud?"

"Yes, ma'am, you sure did."

I was trying to think of a delightful explanation, when a loud noise from the direction of the woods caught my attention. A white rabbit hopped out onto the paved parking area and toward where we stood. Seconds later, Mr. McDuffy came charging out after the creature.

"Git back 'ere, you mutinous wee barl av fur!" Duffy yelled. His short legs were pumping hard, his face red from the exertion, but there was no way he would ever catch the bunny.

Without a second thought, I took off after the cute critter. I managed to head it off near the entrance of the museum, and seconds later scooped it up.

"Thanks for catchin' me wayward varmint," Duffy said, as he reached to take the animal.

I moved so he couldn't get it. "What are you going

to do with him?"

"Take him back wha he belongs. Now gie it ter me!!"

I backed away from Duffy's hands. "Not until you tell me what you want with him."

Duffy sighed. "Yer are a pain in de arse, ain't yer lassie?"

"You're not making stew with this cute little guy?"

Duffy let out what sounded like some not very nice Celtic language. "I'm not gonna cook Leonardo."

Hunter had come over to stand next to me, and a snort came from his direction.

"Don't yer laugh, outsider." Duffy glared at Hunter.

"Sorry."

"So what are you going to do with him?" I asked.

Duffy looked down for a time before he met my gaze. "'e's me pet."

That didn't satisfy me in the least. "Then why was he running from you?"

"He likes ter run."

"I don't think so."

"Give me rabbit back." Duffy tried again to take the bunny from my arms.

"No!" I turned away from him, brushing against Hunter.

"Aren't you being a little harsh?" Hunter whispered. "Rabbits run if they get half a chance."

"Not this one," I told him, though I'd have a hard time explaining that

Leonardo had told me he didn't want Duffy to take him.

"Women," Hunter muttered.

Okay, now I wanted to smack both men upside their hard, stubborn heads. I clinched my teeth and pulled the rabbit closer to me.

"Fine, I'll tell yer." Duffy looked at his feet for a minute before he glanced at me again.

I looked at Duffy and waited for his explanation.

"He's sweet on a lassie."

My patience was at the end of its rope and ready to hang somebody. "And?"

Duffy's cheeks went pink. "Yer take a lad bunny and a lassie bunny, and next yer 'av bunny babies al' over de place."

I looked at the fur-ball in my arms, forcing his little face around to look at me. "Is this true?"

"You're seriously asking the rabbit?" Hunter's voice was a combination of humor and bewilderment.

I ignored the human and handed the bunny to the leprechaun. "Behave, Leonardo."

The pair headed back into the woods.

I turned and met Hunter's amused expression. "So the rabbits talk to you, huh?"

He should be grateful I didn't bite him. "Would you believe me if I said they do?"

"No."

I shrugged. "Since that's settled, don't you have work to do?"

"You're right." He gave me a look of total exasperation and stalked off.

"Bonehead," I muttered as I followed.

He didn't look back, but he chuckled.

Chapter Four

I sat on my haunches nose—to-nose with my nemesis. He was much smaller than me, an easily taken foe if I chose to go all-out. I'm pretty sure he didn't believe that. Nevertheless, it was the truth. His sparkling emerald gaze held mine as we assessed each other, each of us wondering how the game would be played.

It was he who struck first, his weapon sharp, his aim exact. I easily dodged the blow, and followed up by edging toward him. As expected he backed up, but then threw himself forward like a spring. I was expecting move, but it was a fluid motion that came closer than I'd like to his target. He was quite skillful.

The sound of a vehicle pulling in distracted me for a second. My opponent took the opportunity to strike, and he came within a hair's breadth of my nose. I parried, following that with a tip of my head in appreciation of his ability. The game was over, though. We both knew who had just pulled in my yard.

I barked, and he arched his back and hissed. I barked again, and he let out a wail. Behind him appeared Miz Carlisle, who scooped my nemesis into her arms.

"What did that mangy mutt do to my little Bumpkins?"

We gave each other one last look of appreciation,

the equivalent of "good game" between two humans, and I loped off toward home.

The minute I was inside, I shifted and pulled on the robe I keep by the back door. I rushed into the living room to find my cousin and her fiancé kissing with an intensity that likely would have embarrassed me, had I been totally human. "Okay, okay, you can do that later," I told them. "Right now I have to know how it went."

They were in no hurry to break up their necking session, so I stood, arms crossed, waiting for them to cool down. I finally decided the display was too much even for a half-canine, and went into my bedroom to put on clothes. When I came back, Ace and Shay had moved from kissing to staring into each other's eyes. "Okay, so you had a wonderful time and you came back here to rub it in my face. Am I close?"

Shay looked at me. "Sorry, cuz. Yes, we had a wonderful time. We came back because we have lives."

"My parents loved her." Ace's face brightened with pride. "I knew they would."

"Get any writing done?" I asked her.

Shay sighed. "Of course not. I don't know why I even took my laptop."

"That just proves you had a good time. I'm glad. You both needed a break." They were good people and they deserved happiness.

"So what did you do while we were gone?" Ace asked.

I shrugged. "Just wrote, mostly."

Shay leaned back, hands on her heart, eyes so wide I thought they might pop out. "Oh Lord, how many books did you write?"

I gave Shay a wide-eyed, innocent look and exaggerated wildly. "Only three."

She rolled her eyes. "You need a hobby."

"Ha-ha. I bit back the grin as the two of us grabbed iced tea and cookies from the kitchen and took the snack into the living room. It was so much fun to tease Shay, and she loved to tease me too. She was also supportive, and I considered popping out with the bestseller list thing, but I didn't want to do anything to lessen her happiness. She would be there for me if I really needed her. Either of them would be. Ace was like a brother to me, and I loved them both.

The lovebirds sat side-by-side on the couch, and I curled my legs under me in one of the comfy chairs. They were adorable, and I worked hard at not being jealous.

It seems to me sometimes that I got a sour deal with the shapeshifting. Not that I would change who I am, I love being able to shift. It was only when it came to relationships, of all kinds, that things got dicey. I couldn't exactly announce to all and sundry that I'm half-collie. Only family and one of my closest friends know my secret, and I trusted her because she had a secret of her own. Thing is, if I couldn't open up to my friends, how could I open up to a casual date? Or even a guy I was falling for? But how could anybody know the real me without knowing what I am? That leaves me exactly where?

Then again, who was I really? A writer? A collie? A hermit who only goes out to run around the yard, buy necessities, or write at the library? Where I meet arrogant professors doing research. I smiled, remembering the tall handsome pain in the rear. "While you were gone I helped out a fellow writer do research."

Shay smiled. "Sleuth Dog has Internet skills."

Sleuth Dog. Shay calls me that when I use my doggie self to infiltrate and gather information. People never pay attention what they say in front of a dog, and dogs have excellent hearing. I think the whole thing is amusing, but this wasn't about that.

"Actually, there's a guy in town who's writing a book on Ugly Creek history, and I've been showing him around."

"Wait, did you say 'guy'?"

I sighed. "Yes, he's male. A professor at some little private college."

"Old dude?" she asked.

"No, I'd say maybe a little older than me. Opinionated like you wouldn't believe."

"It's not Hunter Devereux, is it?"

I couldn't have been more surprised if Ace had told me he was a were-giraffe. "How did you know that?"

He shrugged. "I did a magazine series with him about four years ago. We went to South America to do a piece on the impact of deforestation on endangered species of the rainforest. He and another guy wrote the articles, and I took the photos. It was an incredible place, and we had an amazing time." Ace's shoulders relaxed, and a smile lit his face.

"You'll have to tell me what it was like down there," Shay said. "Was it scary?"

"Some of it was," he said.

"I would love to hear all about it too, but right now I *have* to know why you thought of some random guy you did a job with instead of all the other people in the world."

Ace grinned. "Because he's the reason I moved to Ugly Creek."

"You're making less sense all the time." I told him.

He chuckled. "Okay, it's like this. Hunter was a little obsessed with Ugly Creek, even brought along some material about it that he'd printed off the Net. He swore he would write a fascinating history of the area."

My curiosity was twitching with interest. "Did he say what it was that interested him so much?"

"Not really. He just said it was a different kind of place." Ace grinned. "Got me interested, and after I got back to the States I did some research of my own."

"And here you are." Shay smiled at him with that wide-eyed, every-word-he says-is-interesting expression only a woman in love gets.

"He's definitely opinionated about fiction," I said.

Ace grinned. "Hunter is a little bit odd."

"Odd how?" Shay asked.

"He's a nerd. Loves fantasy and science fiction."

Understanding dawned, alone with a desire to smack myself on the forehead. "That's why the bow ties."

Ace laughed. "Has he worn a fez yet? Bow ties aren't so bad. Funky red hats are a little weirder. I tried to talk to him, but he wouldn't listen. I finally got so frustrated I hid his fez."

Shay smacked him on the arm. "That's not nice."

He made a scoffing noise. "You try taking pictures while laughing. Plus, I think he scared the animals."

"Were there any women out there with you?" Shay narrowed her eyes at him.

"Two, but they were ugly and we all started

stinking pretty quick."

"You're lying," she told him. "I'll bet they were gorgeous."

I rolled my eyes at the couple then headed toward my bedroom. Those two were cute, but I had some serious thinking to do. I had made a deal with a man I didn't know or trust to help me save my career—a career he didn't seem to have a lot of respect for. I don't mind strange, kind of like it, as a matter of fact, but a grown man who was so caught up in his own world he wore bow ties every day? Who liked to wear a fez? That might be a little too weird even for me. Maybe.

So the bow ties were probably a nerdy thing. I'd figured it was fifty-fifty nerd or weird professor style. Maybe it was both.

I thought about Hunter in a fez—a hat that looked a lot like a cardboard toilet paper tube, size adjusted to fit a human head, capped at the top and painted red. Actually, it was way too easy to form the mental picture. He was different, and I liked different. Except for the whole lack of respect for how I made my living thing. That irritated me, like a flea crawling around on my neck.

Scrappy was curled on my bed.

"I'm an idiot," I told her.

She looked at me for a minute, then went back to washing her face.

I pulled out a new writers' magazine and sprawled beside her.

Chapter Five

"This is called Ghost Hill? Seriously?" Hunter narrowed his eyes at me as if wondering whether I was teasing him.

"It's what the locals call it."

"Well, there is a hill."

I shrugged. "There's been a lot of paranormal activity reported here. Lots of sightings and such."

He groaned, and I gave him my most innocent expression. "Hey, you're the one who wants to debunk all those wild stories."

"Something tells me you don't think I can."

What I thought was the least of his problems, but I couldn't exactly tell him that. "Not really, no."

He gave me a measuring look. "You want to believe."

I snorted and my face heated. "Want has nothing to do with it."

He groaned. "Please tell me you don't believe in that Bigfoot bunk. Or the aliens. Or—"

"Faeries, leprechauns, and shapeshifters."

"I haven't heard anything about shapeshifters, but yeah. Please tell me you don't believe, cute stuff."

I patted his cheek. "Sure. I don't believe."

I walked a few steps away before looking over my shoulder. "Oh, I forgot unicorns." I grinned as I continued over to the back edge of the hill. I glanced back again, and saw his frustrated glare. He did not like to be teased, at least about the paranormal. Well that was interesting and offered a wide range of possibilities for fun.

He eventually wandered my way, and a few minutes later, he gave up being grouchy and spoke. "This is Sawyer Hill, isn't it?"

I nodded. "This is it, the place where Neil Sawyer built the very first European-type person's house in Ugly Creek. Over there is what's left of the foundation." We walked over to where hand-worked rocks, now aged and weathered, outlined the perimeter of what had been a small house.

"This was the first house, but the Sawyer guy wasn't the founder of the town?"

"No, he was just the first to build a house." I shrugged. "I don't know how that works. Probably some paperwork thing."

"Most likely."

Hunter took notes, snapped pictures, and gave me occasional sideways looks, probably to make sure I wasn't going to try to fake something weird. Not that I'd have to fake it.

I enjoyed feeling the wind in my hair. A grasshopper leaped near me and I shivered with the desire to shift and play. What would the intrepid writer do if Trixie just appeared out of nowhere?

I glanced back at Hunter, who was sitting on his heels so he could examine the blocks better. There were no weeds in this area, only grass that had been cut and maintained, which led me to believe there were those in Ugly Creek who understood the benefit of keeping historical spots spruced up. For pride or tourists, I couldn't say. Either way, it made me proud of the quirky little town.

A few minutes later, I caught a glimpse of a beautiful young woman near the line of trees on the far side of the hill. She turned and I saw a pair of bright blue wings. Excitement rushed through me, and I glanced toward where Hunter was occupied taking photos of some gorgeous wild blue sage and tall purple ironweed. Before I could go toward her, the woman took flight. With one quick flash of color, she was gone.

My first thought was to rush over to Hunter and tell him what I'd seen. Before I could do that, I was hit with a sudden, thick dose of reality. Who was I to reveal Ugly Creek secrets to a man I barely knew? Or anybody for that matter? I was an outsider myself, accepted here because my aunt lived here. She told me about the specialness of Ugly Creek because of my own secret. She'd confided in me and had made it very clear that I was to protect the creatures that lived here. Ugly Creek was a sanctuary, and I was welcome. That didn't mean I had the right to share with a complete outsider just because I wanted to burst his arrogant little bubble.

I knew all that. When I had agreed to show Hunter around, I took seriously my role as protector of this little town that had so generously accepted me as I am. I didn't want to violate their privacy. I actually wasn't thinking of it that way. I was only thinking what it would be like for snobby professor dude to discover just how wrong he was about things he couldn't understand. Maybe he'd be a little more open-minded afterward.

Well, that dose of reality put a fine dent in my fun.

I wandered back over to tall, dork, and unbelieving. He was still taking photos and writing in his little notebook, so I walked around some more, wishing once again that I could shift and play in the sun.

My super-canine hearing meant I heard the rough sound of the motor before the human did. I leaned my head and listened. Motorcycle, Harley if I wasn't mistaken. I'm sure there are a few Harley bikes in and around Ugly Creek, not to mention tourists and visitors. Still, I was fairly sure what I was hearing was the sound of the bike belonging to the most well-known and well-loved person in Ugly Creek.

By the time the motorcycle topped the hill, Hunter had stopped his exploration and was watching the same place I was. The bike stopped, and the diminutive rider swung off the seat. The woman was dressed in black leather, her dark brown hair had streaks of gray, her face had only a few wrinkles, but her eyes held the wisdom of years. Nobody knew just how old she really was, but it was universally accepted that she'd been around for quite some time.

Respect and affection filled my heart as I hurried to her for a hug. "It's so good to see you, Aunt Octavia!"

"It's good to see you too, little one."

I laughed. "You don't come up to my chin."

"Physical size is irrelevant," she said, as she took my hand in hers and rubbed her forefinger over the palm.

"Anything interesting?"

"With you, always." She raised her head and scrutinized Hunter. "But first we must deal with Mr. Skeptic over here."

He held out his hand. "Hunter Devereux. It's a

pleasure to meet you Ms...."

Instead of shaking his hand, she turned it palm up and was rubbing the tips of her fingers over it. "Call me Aunt Octavia, everybody does."

He was frowning. "May I ask what you're doing, um, Aunt Octavia?"

"Listening to the spirits."

"Do the spirits speak to you a lot?"

"The spirits speak to all of us, but most people don't stop to listen."

"What are they saying about me?"

She held his hand in both of hers and smiled. "To be careful what you ask for, you might get the truth."

He laughed, the jack in the literary box actually laughed at Aunt Octavia. My breath caught in my throat as I waited for the spirits to send lightning, or for Aunt Octavia to kick his ass, whatever came first.

She only smiled. "Heed the warning or not, your choice."

"That was a pretty vague warning, don't you think, Yoda? Why not give me something solid to work with."

"As you wish." She rubbed his palm with her fingertips again.

"I thought you psychics just looked at palms, not rubbed them."

"I do as I was taught."

"So you learned to read palms, uh? Let me guess, you're a gypsy?"

She looked up then, directly into his eyes. He closed his mouth and his gaze held tightly with hers.

"Whatever you learn here, whatever you do, it will make no difference," she said. "He will only respect your choices when you show your true self to him."

She let go of his hand and started back my way.

He took a stumbling step, then stopped. "How did you…who told you…who the hell are you?"

Aunt Octavia stopped beside me. "Trust your gift." She smiled. "And your heart." She got on her Harley and headed out.

As the motor noise decreased, Hunter came up beside me. "What the hell are you trying to pull having your aunt, or whoever the hell she is, show up and spit out just enough to make a lesser man believe she is more than just a con artist?"

My hands gripped into fists, and I'm pretty sure fire came out my nose. "I know you don't believe in what you can't put in a test tube, but she's the real thing."

"Is she?"

I so wanted to knock the crap out of this jerk. My fingers tightened to remind me they were more than ready to do just that. "You are the most arrogant son of rock moss that I've ever met. You can find your own people and places to insult." I turned to leave, but a thought had me turning back. "And I don't give a flying tree mite what you think about my books. You wouldn't know a good story if it bit you on your nose." With that I stomped off toward the trail that led down to my car.

I jerked open my car door and slid inside. It wasn't until I was out on the main road and headed toward home when I allowed myself a tiny smile. He'd called me cute. Didn't make up for insulting one of the wisest, and nicest, people I know. A person everybody respected. Still, I'd enjoyed hearing it.

Damn, I'm pathetic.

****

Shay and Ace were in the kitchen, but I blew right past them in my urgency to run outside. I couldn't seem to speak, so I simply turned my back as I undressed. Ace's groan followed me as I shifted into Trixie and blew through the doggy door. Behind me I heard Shay say something about me not even noticing the food.

Finally I was free to allow my body to fly across the ground. I swung toward one side of the yard, then loped as fast as I could straight at the other side. My fur flew in the wind, and my long ears flopped gently. It was a rush like no other. I pushed hard, letting the exertion work lose the knotted stress in my body.

Bumpkins stalked over to the fence, and I growled. His eyes widened and he turned back toward his house. Good, I didn't feel like playing. All I wanted to do was to beat on one handsome man who harbored an ego the size of the Atlantic Ocean.

Either that or kiss him.

I growled and took off running again. Why in the world did I think I could consort with a snobby professor type? Even if he was a fine specimen of human male.

When I couldn't run anymore, I headed back into the house. I didn't bother to shift, just went directly to my bedroom as Trixie. There I put on a robe, gathered clothes, and headed to the shower.

By the time I got a plate of meatloaf and potatoes, I felt like a different person. Shay and Ace were sitting on the couch talking, their empty plates lingering on the coffee table. They each glanced my way with a small smile, but neither spoke. Understandable, I owed them an apology and an explanation. "I'm sorry, Ace. My intention was not to embarrass either of us."

He nodded without looking at me.

"Are you all right?" Shay asked. "I've never known you to pass right by food like that, especially meat."

Warm-fuzzies tickled me. My cousin was such a sweet woman, and she honestly cared about me. "I'm okay, I just had to run long and hard enough to get past an insatiable desire to beat a bow tie wearing professor over the head, that's all.

Ace looked at me then. "Hunter? What did he do?"

"He insulted Aunt Octavia."

Two pairs of eyes all but popped out of their heads.

"He must either be totally bonkers, or has a death wish," Shay said.

"He just doesn't believe anything he can't fit in his little world of 'science knows it all'," I told her. "She told him to be careful what he asked for, he might get the truth."

Ace frowned. "That upset him?"

I wasn't sure I should go on, but I couldn't seem to stop my mouth. "He asked for something more specific, and she told him nothing he discovered here would change how 'he' whoever that is, thought about Hunter. Bow tie freaked, but Aunt Octavia calmly walked over to me and told me to trust my gift and my heart, then she got on her bike and left.

"Hunter accused me of researching him and passing along info to trick him." I shook my head. "I think he may have a few issues."

"His dad."

Shay and I both looked at Ace. "What are you talking about?" she asked.

"His issues," I said. "They're what his dad thinks

44

about him?"

Ace nodded. "His dad's straight-laced and cold. From the little Hunter said, the man never gave him any real caring or understanding."

Well, things were almost making sense. "Why would finding something here have anything at all to do with Hunter's relationship with his father?"

Ace shrugged. "He's writing a book about Ugly Creek, right? What would that have to do with what anybody thinks about him?"

"Did you ever figure out why he was so fascinated by this area?" Shay asked.

"Not really." Ace's forehead tightened in thought. "He did say something about the high number of supernatural tales, I suppose that could be why he was drawn here. There's gotta be more than that, though."

"Makes sense to me," I said. "The more supernatural tales, the more there are to debunk."

Ace's frown deepened. "He's debunking?"

"That's what he wants to do. Not that he really can. Not here."

Ace shifted in his seat. "Maybe that's the point? Maybe he wants to prove the existence of the supernatural."

Shay gasped. "That would not be good. Ugly Creek's secrets need to stay hidden."

"Trust me," I said. "He's a nonbeliever and he wants to make sure he shows the whole world he's right."

"That makes no sense. He always seemed open to anything. After all, he writes—" Ace leaned back, eyes closed, hand over mouth.

"Writes what?" I put all the demand I could into

my voice.

"He'll kill me."

I leaned forward in my chair. "If you don't tell us, *I'll* kill you."

"I'll help her," Shay said.

He groaned mightily. "Magical Realism," he said, then put both hands over his mouth.

"That doesn't mean he actually believes in magic or whatever."

Ace sat up and looked his fiancée in the eye. "I seriously don't see how he can write what he does and not at least be open to the possibilities. That's what may have attracted him to Ugly Creek, the possibility of the concrete reality of the paranormal."

"That doesn't mean he believes in the supernatural." Shay was looking at Ace wide-eyed.

Ace held her gaze. "It's possible all this talk about not believing and debunking is a cover for what he really wants, to prove the supernatural is real?"

Shay bounced a little and grabbed Ace's shoulder. "Oh, that makes so much sense."

"It does, doesn't it?" Ace grinned.

I heard what they said, but all I could think of was one thing. "That sanctimonious jerk writes genre!"

Chapter Six

I raced around the yard in an effort to disperse some of the bottled-up energy from a long morning of writing, deleting, writing, deleting, finally writing a sentence that worked. Make a cup of tea. Repeat. The canine side of me loves to move and the human world is just not active enough to keep that side of me happy. Or maybe I just love to shift into a dog and run until I'm so tired I'm ready for a nap. I could use one after a sleepless night and a morning filled with non-productive writing. This was not at all like me. I sleep well, wake up ready to go, and always have a couple thousand words done before daylight.

It was all the men's fault. Ace because he wouldn't tell us Hunter's pseudonym, and Hunter's because he was a jerk. I growled at a stick, pawed it around, and growled at it some more. That helped.

The sound of a vehicle pulling off the road had me curious, and I ran around to see what was up. The car was familiar. Hunter. I growled a little just for the hell of it.

He headed toward house, and I arranged to get there just as he arrived at the porch steps. He smiled when he saw me. "You must be Terri's collie. You're a gorgeous girl."

I watched and waited. It was amazing what a human will say to a dog, and this might be interesting.

He reached out a hand, and I sniffed it with interest. Coffee, eggs and bacon, toast, soap, new book. Interesting. He touched my head. "You're a sweet dog, aren't you? Maybe you could put in a good word for me with your owner. I don't think she likes me much. I know I can be opinionated. I upset her badly with the psychic woman thing. Those people must be questioned. We can't be sucked into nicely worded platitudes spoken in order to convince us—"

I growled, and he jumped back. Smiling to myself, I headed toward the back door.

By the time I got dressed and reached the front door, he'd knocked twice. Impatient varmint. I opened the door.

"Good morning, Terri."

"Hunter."

His smile was big and sure of itself. "I have come to apologize to m'lady for my opinionated remarks yesterday. I really must learn to be more accepting of other people's views."

With both hands, I grabbed Mr. Snob by the collar and pulled him into the house, it wasn't hard, he didn't pull back at all. I kicked the door closed behind me and let go of the crisp, white collars of his shirt, leaving him mussed and wrinkled. His eyes had all but popped out of his head.

"Look, you overgrown pond scum." I poked him with my finger to drive home the point. "I don't give a flea's ass what you say to me. It's when you insult one of the wisest, nicest, most giving people I've ever met that you get me upset. You can question all you want, and I'm sure Aunt Octavia would be happy to discuss her ability with you. It's when you get all smarter-than-thou with a woman who knew more before she was born than either of us will ever know that you make me want to use your head to practice pounding in nails. Understand, or do you need bigger words?"

I took one step back, holding him with my glare. For a moment I was a little concerned he might faint or something equally pathetic, instead he closed his eyes and let his head drop forward. After a moment, there was a big sigh, and he met my gaze. "Was I that bad?"

"Worse."

He sighed again and dropped into the nearest chair. "So I've lowered myself to the point of insulting eccentric old ladies. Whatever you want to do to me, Terri. Go ahead, I deserve it."

There's not really a smell of sincerity, but the scent that came off Hunter was the closest I'd ever encountered. I sighed. "You have no idea how you come across to other people, do you?"

"Apparently not."

I sat on the edge of the couch, facing him. "I don't understand why you have your knickers in a wad over the supernatural stuff in Ugly Creek. What difference does it make whether it's true or not? What business is it of yours either way?"

"You got me, it's not. I told myself that I was trying to protect unwary people from losing their money to crooks—"

"Nobody asked for any damn money."

"I know, Terri. It was just all I had."

"Except for the truth."

His gaze was on his shoes as he nodded. "Except for that."

"You're trying to impress somebody. I'd guess the

'he' Aunt Octavia was talking about."

He met my gaze then, and there was pain there. "Yeah. If you didn't tell her anything, then she found out some other way that my dad and I don't get along."

"Because she has nothing better to do than research random people just so she can put on a private show for no apparent reason."

"The alternative is…disconcerting."

"And by disconcerting, you mean scares the pee out of you."

He laughed. "I love the way you just come out and say it like you see it."

I touched his knee. "Tell me about your dad."

His lips slowly pulled into a smile. "I'm sitting in your living room and you want to talk about my dad. Not the subject I'd most like to discuss with a beautiful woman."

He'd called me beautiful. My inner cheerleaders were shouting and dancing and shaking pompoms for all they were worth. I let them continue their fun as I smiled at the nice man. "Please. I want to understand."

He shrugged. "I'm an overachiever determined to please my overachieving parents, especially my dad."

I realized I was thirsty, and could hear my mom's voice reminding me that hospitality was important to humans. "Would you like some sweet tea?"

"I'd love some." There was relief in that voice. Happy for the reprieve, or was his mouth dry. Both, probably.

He followed me into the kitchen. I was pouring the tea when I saw him giving a platter on the table a longing look. "Is it too early for sweets?" I asked.

"Never."

"They're homemade. Shay and I love making cookies."

He grinned. "I prefer eating cookies."

I grinned back. "Grab the platter and we'll relax in the living room."

We nibbled cookies and sipped tea for a while before Hunter finally spoke again.

"Dad is a law professor at Emory University."

"Georgia? I thought you're from Memphis."

"Born and lived in Tennessee until my teens, when Dad landed a professorship at Emory and we moved to Georgia. My parents live in Atlanta now."

"Your dad sounds like a pretty serious guy."

"Very serious."

"I'll bet he wanted his son to go into law."

"Wanted isn't the word. Expected is more the truth."

"What about your mom?"

"She usually goes along with Dad. I don't blame her, it's easier that way."

"Is she a professional too?"

"She's a high school history teacher."

"And neither one of them would even consider something like Bigfoot could exist."

He snorted. "You think I'm opinionated, you should hear my dad."

"So, you think that if you prove Ugly Creek is paranormal-free, your Dad will be proud of you?"

He cringed. "Well, when you say it like that..."

"Have you considered doing what Auntie O. says and just show him the real you?"

He looked like I'd just told him to walk naked into a freezer and lock the door. "I'd like to keep my head, thank you."

"Maybe he'd understand."

"Yeah, and maybe a flock of geese will fly to the moon. Not possible."

All at once, laughter poured out of me. "So you Devereux men are the most stubborn creatures on the face of the earth."

He leaned back and laughed with me. "It's entirely possible."

I munched on a cookie as I considered that maybe this man wasn't quite as weird as I thought he was. I noticed his bow tie was skewed, and I reached over to straighten it out. His breath sucked in, and I froze. "Did I hurt you?"

"No." He caught my hand and held it. "You know, I really did come by here to apologize. I know I was out of line yesterday. If you'll tell me where to find your aunt, I'll apologize to her also."

"She's not my aunt, everybody just calls her that. I have no idea where she lives either, I don't think anybody does. She just shows up where she's needed."

There was excitement in his eyes. "Interesting character."

"Very." There was an instant connection between us, an understanding only two writers could experience and share.

"Hopefully I'll run into her." He swallowed and took my hand in both of his. "Would you be willing to point me in the direction of interesting places in Ugly Creek, even if I am pond scum?"

I narrowed my eyes at him. "Are you still planning to prove there is nothing super or para here?"

"I'm not planning anything right now. All I know

is that I have a contract to write a book about Ugly Creek, and I could think of worse things to spend my time doing."

I considered my options. "You could check out the Eaglehair house. It's where the original town charter was written. The council met there for years."

"And?"

I lowered my chin and looked up at him with a wide-eyed, innocent expression. "And it's supposed to be haunted."

He groaned and dropped his head into his hands. "You don't know when to quit, do you?"

"I hate to tell you this, handsome, but pretty much anyplace in this town has a hard-to-explain story of some sort."

He raised his head, his hazel eyes filled with curiosity. "Did you just call me handsome?"

I made a point of rolling my eyes. "Yes, but if you tell anybody I'll deny it happened."

He grinned. "Sure thing, gorgeous."

My chin dropped, and I knew my mouth was hanging open, but I was so shocked I seriously could not move.

With the tip of his finger, Hunter pushed up on my chin. He leaned toward me ever so slightly. I stopped breathing. My heart did some kind of funky thing like a butterfly slammed into me.

He blinked as though awakening and looked at his watch. "I have an interview with the mayor. I'd better get going."

Think! I ordered my brain. "She's nice."

"With a name like Paradise, I guess she has a lot to live up to."

I nodded, though I wasn't sure I understood what he'd just said.

He took my hand and pulled me to my feet. "So you'll meet me at this Eaglehair house tomorrow?"

"Yeah, at ten?"

"Sounds good." We were on the porch by this time. He brushed a lock of my hair off my face. "See you in the morning."

"Okay."

He leaned toward me again, but this time he didn't stop until his lips pressed firmly against mine. He pulled back and whispered, "See you tomorrow." Then he went down the steps and out to his car.

I watched as he pulled away, not sure what to make of the man or the feelings he stirred up in me.

"I've never seen him before," Miz C said, her words too soft to be heard by a human ear. "Wonder where he came from."

"His name is Hunter Devereux. He's a writer working on a history of Ugly Creek."

Her eyes went wide, likely shocked to hear her barely spoken question answered. For a second she froze, then she seemed to decide to go with the flow. "He's a friend of yours?"

"Yes, he is." I smiled as I turned and headed back into the house. What a day!

And it wasn't even lunchtime yet.

Chapter Seven

The Eaglehair house was a plain, white, two-story wooden building. The rectangular structure wasn't much to look at, sort of a tall box with several windows, a stone foundation, stone chimney on one side, a few wooden steps leading to the front door, three windows on each floor. It looked more like a shoebox than a historically important piece of architecture built in 1774.

"So this is it, huh?"

"Yep."

Hunter and I were standing in front of the house, gazing up at its total lack of interesting features. It was nine forty-five, and the morning sun was struggling to peer through a thick bank of dark clouds. Cold air blew through the trees and I shivered even through my light jacket. Damn thin Florida blood!

Hunter put his jacket around my shoulders. The fabric still carried warmth and a masculine, spicy scent. "You don't have to lend me this," I told him.

He shrugged. "I'm not cold."

I decided to change the subject. "Sally said that she would be here at ten."

"So this isn't a tourist thing where the house is open regular hours?"

"Not really. Sally gives tours for groups and stuff, but mostly she just takes care of the place."

"Sounds like lost income to me. I didn't even know the house was still here and that it's possible to go in."

I smiled. "I told you there are a lot of weird tales that come out of this place. Maybe they spread those stories because they want to scare the visitors away."

He snorted. "More likely the stories are to increase the number of tourists."

"Except they don't advertise the house."

He tightened his mouth as he frowned. "I'm still working on that."

A tall, middle-aged woman with a long black braid that bounced against her back as she rushed across the street. "Hope you haven't been waiting long, I was talking to old Lou Ferguson, and he doesn't know when to shut up." She stuck out a hand to Hunter. "Hey, I'm Sally Eaglehair. You must be that city slicker who's interested in our quiet little slice of God's green earth."

"Hunter Devereux, and from what I've heard, this slice isn't necessarily quiet."

I loved Sally's laugh, and today was no exception. Bright, full, pitched in an oddly low range for such a pretty woman with a higher-pitched speaking voice.

"I said quiet, not boring. It's always interesting around here, but not in a bad way."

"Your name being Eaglehair, I take it you're related to the original builders of this house?"

Sally nodded as she unlocked the front door. "Distant cousin. There's always somebody to take over care of the house, and this generation it's mine. I love this old place, I'm so glad there wasn't anybody else willing and able. I'd have had to fight for the honor."

As our hostess went into the building, Hunter leaned so his mouth was near my ear. "What do I do if I see a ghost?"

I shrugged. "Say hello?"

He chuckled as he motioned for me to go ahead of him. Gentleman or chicken? I guess we'd see.

Sally handed each of us a booklet. "There's a lot of information in here, more than I give on the tours. We offer them for purchase, in case people want more details. You can look all you want. I'll be around if you have questions."

Hunter had some bills out before I could get my hand in my purse. "Keep the change."

"You didn't have to do that, but thank you very much. The money will go toward upkeep of the house." She was still smiling at him over her shoulder as she left the room.

"I'd have bought my own," I told him.

"You're helping me. It's only fair."

"Sounds reasonable." I turned and started toward the back, his quiet, but deep-pitched laugh following me as I went.

First stop was an old-fashioned parlor. This one, so said the booklet, was where the founders of Ugly Creek met to do the founding way back in 1780. "More than two-hundred years ago."

A strong hand clasped my shoulder. "This is what I love about writing histories. Research."

I smiled into Hunter's handsome face. He was several inches taller than my five-nine, tall enough that I had to look up. Unusual, most men weren't much taller than me "Research is one of my favorite things too."

"Gonna write a two-hundred year-old parlor into one of your books?"

"I might."

He smiled, and my body tingled in reaction. A sudden urgency to kiss the man all but knocked me off my feet. What the hell was wrong with me? I'd never felt this strong a desire in my entire pathetic life. When he turned and walked away, I was relieved I had time and space to get my stupid self together.

I followed him as we explored the rest of the first floor. There was another parlor, a dining area, the door that led to the summer kitchen, which was located outside—without air conditioning it was too hot to cook inside the house during the summer—and a huge ballroom.

We mounted the stairs to the second floor, which, not surprisingly, held bedrooms. There were six, furnished and preserved so they looked like they probably did when the original Eaglehair family lived there. I still had Hunter's jacket around my shoulders, but it kept slipping, so I slid the thing on. The warmth, the spicy smell, the way it was so big it seemed to enclose me in its grasp. I lost myself for a moment to the sensual feel of the garment around me.

A sharp gasp had me spinning around to find Hunter staring at a beautiful young woman standing just inside the open window.

"You startled me," he said. "I didn't know there was anybody else in here."

Her long, straight black hair reached to her waist. A lock of it moved as something bright green waved at her back. Faery. My guess was that she'd come in through the window while neither of us was looking. She looked at Hunter, obvious curiosity in her expression.

"Hi," he took a small step toward her and held out his hand. "My name is Hunter, what's yours?"

Her eyes widened to an unnatural width, and she let out a soft, lyrical call rather like a sigh played on a lyre.

Hunter held up his hands, as if surrendering. "We aren't going to hurt you."

I forced back the strong desire to laugh. Poor Hunter had a faery treed and didn't know what to do with her. Didn't even realize what she was. What was I going to do? I recognized what she was, but not anything about her kind. I did know at least some faeries spoke English. "Hello." I tried to keep my voice quiet and friendly.

She looked at me and blinked, let out another soft, musical sound, then took off out the bedroom door and down the steps. A shimmer followed her, and for a moment it looked like glitter hung in the air. Hunter rushed after her, probably trying to see where she was going. Personally, I was just relieved she hadn't flown out the window.

He turned and looked at me, his expression the textbook version of confused. I smiled in spite of myself. "We got sneaked up on."

"Boy, that's the truth. Good thing she wasn't armed and dangerous."

"Not much dangerous around here, really. Mostly just odd and unexpected."

He glanced toward the door. "I'm beginning to see that."

I put a hand on his arm. "Let's check out the rest of the house."

We explored the other bedrooms, then returned to

the first floor and went down the long stairway to the basement. Rock lined walls were lined with wooden shelves installed on flat pieces of stone built into the wall and jutting out.

"Great job with the stonework."

"I didn't know you were into building."

He sent me a sheepish smile. "Those TV channels that show you how to update and renovate."

"I had to stop watching those shows. It got to where I was actually making plans to buy a house and renovate it."

It was quiet, and when I looked at him I realized he was frowning. "Why didn't you? I don't know you all that well, but I have a suspicion that you would enjoy something like that."

Because I'm a dog. I forced my lips into the form of a smile. "It wouldn't have worked out then."

"Maybe you can one day."

I was saved from further embarrassment by Sally's appearance. "Just checking on y'all and seeing if you have any questions."

Hunter asked intelligent, insightful questions. Okay, I was impressed. Nerdy bow tie or not, the man was deserving of more credit than I'd initially given him. Speaking of which…

The three of us returned to the lobby via another set of stairs, and I took the opportunity to check my idea. "So," I looked up at him through my eyelashes. "What's with the bow tie, anyway?"

He grinned, the varmint. "Bother you, does it?"

I shrugged and gave him my most innocent look. "Not really, just seems a little strange."

"I wear it in honor of my favorite doctor."

I narrowed my eyes. "Who?"

"Exactly."

I chuckled as I shook my head. "You're a mess, Devereux."

"Yep."

When we reached the main floor, Sally said, "If you need more questions answered or to see the house again, just let me know."

"I appreciate you letting me look around."

"Anytime."

We started out, but Hunter stopped. "We saw a young lady upstairs. Is she one of the Eaglehair family?"

For a second, I thought I saw fear in her eyes, then it vanished. "I didn't see anyone. What did she look like?"

"Tall, thin, long dark hair, probably a teenager." He shook his head with a perplexed smile. "She seemed to appear out of nowhere."

Sally shot me a glance that held a question. I moved my chin down in a slight nod, and she turned her gaze back to Hunter. "I don't think I know her. Sometimes local kids come in here to see what the place is like."

"To see if it's haunted?" Hunter asked.

She smiled at that. "They know what we all know, anything can happen in Ugly Creek."

He thanked her again, and Hunter and I walked outside. "Know any good places for lunch?" he asked.

"How about Taco King again, it's not quite two blocks from here."

"Sounds good. I take it you like Mexican food."

A mischievous smile pulled at my lips and I forced

it back. "Are British science fiction shows the best?"

He froze for a heartbeat before a grin lit up his whole face. My breath caught in my throat at how handsome he was.

"So you're a fan?" he asked.

"Not as much as you, but I definitely like the shows."

"Well, British S.F. shows are definitely the best, and I'm buying you lunch. Walk or car?"

I leaned back and studied his face. "So talking British TV makes you pushy?"

His grin pulled even wider. "Sorry."

"No you aren't." I gave his arm a smack.

His grin never faltered. "Okay, I'm not. Do you like other science fiction, or just British TV shows?"

"I watch and read mostly fantasy, but I do like science fiction. I especially love reading the older stuff, Asimov, Bradbury, Clarke."

"Awesome writers. There are some newer authors who look good also."

Like you? "Having time to read has been problematic. I've slipped into a bad magazine habit."

"I don't suppose you mean literary publications?"

"More like celebrity magazines," I whispered.

His eyes opened wide and he gave an exaggerated shiver. "Surely you jest."

"I like seeing what celebrities are up to."

He pulled his face into a thinking expression. "I guess I'll buy you lunch anyway."

I smiled, wide and bright. "It's the least you can do."

He laughed and put his arm around me as we headed toward Taco King. Five minutes later, we stood in front of the ordering window.

"It is my pleasure to buy this beautiful, intelligent lady her lunch," Hunter announced to the teenage order-taker. The boy looked confused, but recovered quickly to take our orders.

A few minutes later, we were sitting at a table in the outside dining area. We were in the shade, and the sunlight made dappled designs on the ground around us. The gentle breeze caught the leaves and their waving, created a moving sensation a bit like rocking gently in a boat.

"These tacos are delicious," Hunter said.

I opened my eyes wide in exaggerated surprise. "And it's not French cuisine."

He leaned his head to one side as if studying me. "Do I really come across as that big a snob?"

"Yes…well…sometimes."

"I'm sorry."

"Mostly you're an okay guy."

He smiled, and his eyes glittered with amusement. "Thanks. I think."

My phone played its quiet bell tune, and I pulled it out of my little, cross-body purse. Very few people had my number, and I didn't recognize the incoming one. I hesitated so long it stopped. Relieved, I started to put it back in my purse. The soft sound of bells sounded again. I surrendered and answered the thing. I might not recognize the number on my phone display, but the voice was familiar. "Hello, Terri girl."

My heart kicked into racing mode. It couldn't be. It was impossible. "Daddy?"

"Yeah, baby, it's me."

I grabbed the edge of my chair and hung on tight.

"Why are you calling me? How did you even get my number?"

"I'm sorry, baby. I wouldn't have called you if I'd had any other choice. I need your help."

It became clear in a flash. He'd left me when I was little, but now, when I had money, he was back. I got to my feet and took a few steps away from the table, turning my back as I went. "You need me, huh? After all these years. So, how much do you need?"

There was a sharp intake of breath. "No! That's not why I'm calling. I don't want or need your money, baby. I can't believe you'd think that, but then again, you don't know me very well."

"Not really, since you left when I was *four*."

"I'm so sorry things played out the way they did. Your mother and I were young and all we could do was muddle through the best we could. I know I hurt you, that was not my intention, baby."

Something snapped. "Don't call me that. You don't have a right to call me baby. You walked away, left Mom and me alone. Left me to deal with what I am all alone."

It was totally quiet for a long moment. "What you *are*? What are you talking about?"

"What do you think? I am your daughter and I got your genes."

"Are you saying you inherited the ability? That can't be. The ability skipped you."

"How would you know? You cut out eight years before I shifted for the first time."

"Because Becky told me you weren't a shifter."

"How could she have told you that when you left before—" Shock cut through me in little shards as I realized what he was saying. "You're lying."

"No, Terri girl, I'm telling you the truth. That's how I have your number. Becky gave it to me in case of emergency."

Tears filled my eyes and I blinked hard to hold them back. "Mom would have told me if she was in contact with you."

"Bab…Terri, I imagine your mom didn't tell you because she was trying to protect you."

"From what?"

A long sigh came through the phone. "You'd have to ask her that."

I'd just about had all the runaround I could take. "What is it you want from me?"

"There's someone who needs your help—not me— and you are the only one who can help her."

"Her? What are you trying to drag me into?"

"It's a long story."

"I'll bet."

"Look, I know this has to be confusing and upsetting. How about I call you again in a couple of days. Let you sort things out a bit."

"I don't need to sort things out."

"Bye, Terri girl. I love you." The line went dead.

I stood looking at my phone as if the thing was responsible for the confusion and pain I felt. What the hell?

I knew one thing for sure, I had to talk to my mom. Unfortunately, she was on a safari halfway around the world, and unreachable for at least another week.

Somehow I turned back to the table and all but collapsed into my seat.

Hunter pulled his chair around so that he was

beside me. He put his hands on my shoulders and gently squeezed. "Are you okay, Terri?"

I wanted to cry like the baby I was the last time I'd heard my father's voice, but I nodded instead. "It was my dad."

"I take it you don't talk to him often."

"Never." People around us were glancing our way. By nature I was a private person, no doubt intensified by the need to keep my ability secret. Coupled with the fact I can hear things a regular human can't—and so I never feel positive about what others can and can't hear—I really don't like sharing in public.

"I don't want to talk about it right now."

"We could go someplace private." He was rubbing his hands up and down my upper arms, like he thought I was about to go into shock or something. Hell, maybe I was.

"I'd like to be alone to think right now."

"I'll go get my car and take you home. We'll get your car later."

"You don't have—"

"I'm not letting you drive. You have no color in your face. I'll be right back. Okay?"

I nodded, he stood, and I watched him go. Once he was gone, I leaned against the back of the chair and stared into my plate. I didn't believe for a minute my Mom had been in touch with my father all these years. She hated the man; why would she contact him?

My mind raced to the day just before my fourth birthday. I'd accidentally seen my dad shift into a big, scary dog. I'd run screaming from the sight into my mother's arms and refused to talk to him. That night my parents had argued. The next day he was gone.

Why would he call me? He said he needed my help. What could he possibly need my help for? For that matter, why would he even think I'd talk to him? I propped my elbows on the table and dropped my head into my hands. My thoughts twisted and flew from one memory to another, one idea to another, one belief to another. What the hell had just happened to my world?

"Terri." Hunter's soft voice and his warm hand against my back comforted me.

I stood and let him lead the way. As we walked he put his arm around me and my mind was racing so fast I leaned into him He got me into his car, and we headed toward Aunt Ruth's house.

He pulled off the road by the front gate, and the first thing I saw was Miz Carlisle in her flower garden. "Of course she's watching us," I muttered. "What else does that nosy old biddy do?"

"She was out there yesterday. So her hobby is watching you?"

I groaned. "Her hobby is flowers. Her fulltime job is making sure nothing happens without her knowing about it, in case she wants to stick her nose in where it isn't wanted."

He tapped his finger under my chin. "Head up, shoulders back, ignore the lowly peasant."

I laughed. Actual laughter. I was amazed.

"Sit right there." He jumped out of the driver's door and a moment later he opened the passenger door and extended his arm to me. "May I escort m'lady?"

"I would be honored, kind sir." I took his arm and we strolled toward the front of the house.

"It is quite a lovely day."

"I agree. The temperature is comfortable, and the

sun is bright and warm." To my right, I could see Miz Carlisle standing in her garden, not even pretending she was interested in anything but us.

When we reached the front door and I extended my key to insert it in the lock, I discovered my hand was still shaking. My face immediately went hot.

"Allow me." Hunter took the key in his hand and made short work of the unlocking. He ushered me inside and closed the door behind us. "That's one very strange neighbor you have over there."

I considered our actions. "And we aren't?"

He made a dismissive motion. "We're writers, we're supposed to be strange."

"You know, I do believe I saw that in my job description."

By this time we were sitting side-by-side on the couch. Hunter brushed a stray strand of my hair off my face and leaned a little closer. "Feeling better?"

I nodded. "Daddy calling me out of the blue like that just shook me up, that's all."

"When was the last time you talked to him?"

"I was four, technically three. It was the day before my birthday."

Hunter sighed. "You haven't heard from him since? Wow."

"I need to think right now. I'm sorry."

"You know, sometimes talking about something will help you get it straight in your head. If you'd like to talk, I'd be happy to listen."

Part of me would like nothing better, but the rest of me was still so confused I'm not sure I could make sense—especially since I wasn't about to tell him what I really was. Whether I liked it or not, my ability was part of this whole, convoluted mess. "I need time to think first, to figure stuff out in my own head. Please."

"Okay. I'm not crazy about leaving you alone, but I understand your need for privacy."

He leaned in and touched his lips to mine, lighting a fire inside me like I'd never experienced. My hands found their way to his shoulders as he wrapped his arms around me and pulled me close. My breasts tingled, I couldn't catch my breath, my heart beat harder than when I was four-legged and racing after a rabbit.

His tongue slipped inside my mouth, and the warm, spicy taste had me losing all thoughts except how amazing this experience was. He moved away, and I fought the need to pull him back to me.

I looked into his eyes, and they'd gone dark, intense, almost scary. "Hunter," I whispered.

"You have my number. If you need anything call, okay?"

I needed him. Now. But I couldn't tell him that, could I? I wasn't sure, and I couldn't think. "Okay."

"I'm meeting the mayor at the courthouse tomorrow morning. She's going to give me a tour and answer questions."

"Sounds interesting." Didn't it?

"I'd like you to go with me."

"Okay." I'd said that too fast, hadn't I? What would he think of me?

"Good. I need you with me in case one of those impossible creatures you believe exists shows up. That way you can call nine-one-one for me."

I smiled. He'd done fine so far by just not believing his own eyes. "I think you'd be all right."

"Maybe." He stood. "I'll pick you up about nine?"

"I'll be ready."

I walked him to the door, where he gave me another incredible kiss. His lips caressed for a moment, then his tongue licked mine, as if leaving a promise. After that, he turned and walked out to his car. One quick wave and he was gone. I closed the door so nosy people couldn't tell how tingly and warm I was. And how badly I wanted to call him back to show me some more magic.

I was so far over my head that I didn't care if I drowned.

Chapter Eight

"The Ugly Creek courthouse was built in 1786. Before that, all the town business was conducted at Amadeus Eaglehair's home." Sophie Paradise, Ugly Creek's mayor spoke with a clear, strong voice that I enjoyed listening to. The woman seemed nice too, and fair.

A few weeks back, Miz Carlisle had tried to run Ace out of town, and the mayor listened to both sides before leading the city council into a vote that protected Ace's dog rescue work. I smiled remembering.

"Has there been much renovation and updating?" Hunter asked.

"Not really," the mayor replied. "We try to keep the authenticity of the building, so we are very careful what type of work we do. There are some things we don't have a choice in, of course. For example, bathrooms were not a part of the original structure. Also, we are proud to be ahead of the game with our facilities for the disabled. But we try to make the changes fit with the original architecture and interior design of the building."

Mayor Paradise moved from where she stood beside a small plaque commemorating the opening of the courthouse and led them down the hall. As you can see, here on the first floor are the public offices like motor vehicle registration, property taxes, marriage licenses and such. My office is also on this floor."

I was admiring the building when I saw her. She was going into one of the office doors, just like everybody else. Except she wasn't like everybody else. She was around three feet tall, had bright red hair, her sparkling dress was bright green, and I could see the trail of golden sparkles from the other side of the huge lobby. This woman had to be a leprechaun.

Now, I was sure Mr. McDuffy was a leprechaun. I'd been told too many times to not believe it. Duffy sure didn't have golden sparkles following him around, and I couldn't begin to explain why the difference.

Neither did I have any idea what this female leprechaun was doing at the courthouse in the middle of a bright, shiny day. Everybody could see her, so why was she taking a chance like that? If these creatures were so impulsive, how was it they were still a secret?

"On the second floor are the courtrooms and judges' chambers," Mayor Paradise was saying. "Let's go up there. Courtroom number one has been kept completely intact just as it was built in 1786."

I glanced back at the sparkling woman just before we headed up the stairs.

Hunter leaned close to my ear. "She's into her character."

I followed his gaze to make sure he was talking about who I thought he was, and sure enough he was.

"Somebody needs to tell her it's not quite Halloween yet." He chuckled softly.

I managed to smile for him, but it was hard for me to understand how he could dismiss something so obviously real as being so mundane as a woman in a costume.

I tried hard to focus on what Mayor Paradise said about the courtrooms and judges' chambers, but my thoughts kept circling from faeries to leprechauns and back to the man beside me. He was so smart, and yet so easily dismissed the obvious.

Within a few minutes, the second floor proved interesting enough to grab my attention. There was hand-crafted furniture, paintings from the eighteenth century and early photographs of stiffly posing men in suits. The fascinating tales Ms. Paradise told about the history of the town, the people, and the courthouse where so many historical events took place.

When we had circled the entire floor, the mayor escorted us back down to the lobby. "Well, I hope you enjoyed my little tour."

"Very much so, Ms. Paradise." Hunter shook the woman's hand. "I really appreciate you taking the time out of your busy day."

"I'm happy to be of assistance, Mr. Devereux. Good luck with your book." She shook my hand too before she headed back to her office.

Hunter turned to me. "Did you enjoy yourself?"

"I did actually." My hand started to rise on its way to caress his cheek, but I realized what was happening in time to convince it to go back to my side where it belonged.

He glanced at the small, hardback notebook in his hand. "I need to go write this stuff down while it's still fresh in my mind, but if you aren't busy, I'd love to take you to dinner later."

I narrowed my eyes. "Dinner, huh?"

"Yep. I've heard there are real restaurants where they serve food on plates. They're supposed to have nice tablecloths and even silverware."

"Really?"

He nodded. "Would you be interested?"

I pretended to think. "On one condition."

"Name it." He sounded cocky, but there was a touch of anxiety in his eyes.

I leaned toward him and whispered. "That they have indoor privies."

It was silly, but we laughed anyway. In fact, we laughed so hard people started to stare, so we hid in a back corner until we got hold of ourselves. When we finally calmed down, we walked out into the lobby.

"May I pick you up at seven tonight?" he asked.

"Sounds good."

We walked together toward the front entrance, Hunter's hand warm and firm against my lower back. Excitement bounced around in my belly. Just before we got to the door, it opened and a tiny woman walked in.

I smiled. "Aunt Octavia!"

She hugged me, then, as usual, took my hand in hers. The tips of her fingers rubbed my palm and I waited for her words of wisdom, and hoped I could eventually sort out what they meant. "Trust all that you are. Those who you need in your life will accept." She looked up and smiled.

Hunter stood close, his gaze down and his expression contrite. When she turned to look at him, he raised his gaze but kept his chin slightly down. "I am very sorry I was so rude to you."

She studied him a moment, then smacked the side of his head. "You're only sorry because you see me as an old woman. I liked you better when you were honest with me."

With that she turned and hurried out the door.

Hunter turned to me, his eyes wide, his jaw slack. I figured I had a similar expression on my face.

"What the hell was that?" he asked.

"Damned if I know."

He looked toward the door and smiled ear-to-ear. "I like that woman."

"Even if she reads palms?"

He shrugged. "I don't care if she reads tea leaves off my head. That woman is awesome."

I was somewhere between confused, delighted, awestruck, and just a tiny bit jealous. How that last got in there, I don't want to consider. "She is pretty cool." Boy was that flat and boring!

He smiled at me, and my heart sang. "Let's get out of here. I have work to do."

"Me too." I'd been forcing myself to continue work on my latest book, even though I still had no idea why my numbers were slipping. Then again, Mr. Ignore-The-Obvious here was supposed to tell me his take on that. I gave him a little "accidental" punch with my elbow, but I couldn't bring myself to ask him. Maybe he was waiting until his research was finished so I wouldn't leave him half-way through. Or maybe it was because he had no frigging idea and couldn't admit it. Or maybe he thought my books were awful and needed to be hidden somewhere they would never be found.

I groaned just about the time we reached our cars. He had taken me to the Eaglehair house earlier so I could get mine, so we stood between where we'd parked our vehicles side-by-side.

"Is something wrong?"

I shook my head, but my gaze was down.

He tipped my chin up. "What did I do?"

The man had a way of making me smile, and I did. "What makes you think the problem is you?"

He shrugged. "Previous experience."

"It's nothing. You've been busy, and you probably don't know what to say, and I've been goofy because of my dad, and it's no big deal if you want to not—"

His lips on mine stopped the babbling. Gee, maybe I should babble more often.

He was smiling when he moved back. "I read your books, went to the store and bought the others, and read them."

"I would have given you copies."

"I wanted to buy them. Plus I didn't want you to know until I was ready to talk with you. Then, with your dad calling and all, I just thought you needed to catch your breath."

"It was that bad?" I closed my eyes and turned my head. "No! Don't tell me."

"I don't buy horrible books."

"But…"

He ran his fingertips down my cheek. "You are an amazing writer and I am honored you asked me for advice."

I looked at my shoes and shrugged. "You're a professor and all, I should be honored."

His warm chuckle washed over me. "A professor who made an ass of himself by insulting you, and your cousin, the very first time we met." He tipped up my chin. "I know I was the choice of desperation, and I want to be damned sure you don't regret asking me."

"But they aren't terrible?" I closed my eyes and groaned. "Gee, could I sound more pathetic?"

"Probably, if you really worked at it."

And once again he had me laughing. "You're a mess, you know that?"

"Yes, actually. My mother informs me of that fact on a regular basis." He leaned in and brushed my forehead with his lips. "Give me a couple more days, and we'll sit down over lunch and see if between us we can get your writing career back to the top where it belongs."

Tears stung my eyes, but I looked up at him anyway. "You really think I can fix what went wrong?"

"I think so. The problem is that we never really know what readers are going to like. The good news is you've been there. They love you. If we can rekindle that love, you'll be on top again."

"Thank you."

"Don't thank me yet, cute stuff." He kissed me soundly, then escorted me to my car door. "I'll see you at seven."

"I'll be waiting." I got in my car and drove toward home, a huge, bright smile pasted on my face all the way there. Even as Trixie, I smiled the whole time I ran around the yard and playing with Scrappy and Bumpkins.

I smiled through my shower and when I lay down for a nap. He liked my books. He liked my books! That thought went with me into sleep, and was there when I woke and got ready for our date. It shouldn't matter what he thought, and yet it did.

Chapter Nine

It was the nineteen-eighties packaged into approximately two-thousand brightly decorated square feet. The delicious smells from a hard-working restaurant kitchen had my mouth watering, and the sound of Eighties pop pouring from the red and stainless steel jukebox in the corner tickled my toes with encouragement to dance. There was even a small dance floor tucked to one side of the tables and chairs.

A jukebox. How cool. A big, vintage, vinyl-playing throwback to another time. There was no need even to put in money. A sign above the machine announced it played Eighties songs constantly while the restaurant was open for business. Scattered over the walls were posters from Eighties' movies and TV shows, heavy on the alien theme.

Waitresses wearing pastel layered tutu skirts, cute sleeveless tops with matching colors, tights that sort-of matched, and fishnet fabric fingerless gloves that almost reached their elbows. Shoes, of course, were black high-top sneakers. It was all part of the delightfully quirky setting at the Alien Station Diner—where the Eighties never ended, and aliens eat for free.

"This place is incredible, how in the world did you find it? I had no idea there was a 1980s-themed restaurant just a couple of miles from Ugly Creek."

"A few weeks ago, as I was planning my trip here,

I saw a notice on the Internet about it. I believe it's fairly new."

The waitress put plates in front of each of us. "Here are your burgers and fries."

"I was wondering how many free meals you serve?" Hunter asked her.

The pretty blond, who looked to be in her early twenties, never missed a beat. "Usually a couple a month, but sometimes there are several within three or four days. Anything else I can get you?"

We both declined, and she went back to her other customers.

Hunter leaned across the table toward me and lowered his voice. "I just want to know one thing."

"What's that?"

"How the hell do you prove you're an alien?"

I held my hands palms up and shrugged. "Green-blood card?"

It was corny, and we both laughed. Still, I wondered if the waitress might be telling at least some form of the truth.

We talked and laughed, and listened to Eighties' songs.

"I love this song," I said, just as he said, "Awesome song!"

It was simultaneous, and startling. Laughter blew through us.

"So you like the group Celebration?" he asked.

"Yes, I do. And that's my favorite Celebration song."

"Mine too." He ginned, his eyes glinting with what looked like mischievousness. "We have a song."

I leaned back in my chair and studied Hunter's

face. "Don't we have to be a couple to have a song?"

"Define couple."

"Two people who are…" I couldn't think of one word I wanted to say I front of him. My face went hot, and I considered climbing under the table.

"I'd say 'two' is the operative word here. There are two of us."

"But we aren't…"

"This is a date, so we are in fact, a dating couple."

My slow brain kicked in. "One date doesn't mean we're a 'dating couple'. We're just two people who went on one date."

"So, we'd have to what, go on more dates, sleep together, get engaged?"

I groaned. "I don't know."

"You were the one questioning whether or not we are a couple. There must be some criteria you based that question on."

"I just never thought of us as couple material."

He grinned. "Stuffy professor and gorgeous author of women's fiction find love in the oddest little town east of anywhere. Too off-the-wall for you?"

"Gorgeous?" I squeaked.

Hunter's grin grew. "Yes, you are. Am I stuffy?"

I shook my head. "Kinda, no, sometimes." I literally bit my tongue to keep from asking, but the word slipped out anyway, "Love?" I dropped my face into my hands and mentally called for Scotty to beam me up. To anywhere but the diner.

"Do you have something against love, my gorgeous dating companion?"

I managed to shake my head.

"How about dropping the uncomfortable word

discussion. We could simply see each other exclusively. Unless that would be a problem?"

I forced myself to look into his eyes. The smile was gone, in its place was a serious expression that shocked me to my bones. "What is it you want, Hunter?"

He reached across the table and took my hands in his. "You fascinate me, Terri Quinn. I want to get to know you better, and the best way to do that is to spend time with you. Being selfish as well as stuffy, I'd like to keep you all to myself."

"And when you go home?"

He gave a little one-shouldered shrug. "First of all, I am in no hurry to leave this interesting town, or you." He squeezed my hands as he smiled. "Second, we can reevaluate the situation when that time comes."

I studied his face for a time. "You like to keep me off kilter, don't you?"

He grinned. "Well, yeah." He squeezed my hands. "This is about getting to know each other. We seem to enjoy each other's company, we like a lot of the same things, we have fun together. I would honestly like to know where that might lead."

I wasn't sure if the chill was one of fear or hope, but it was attention-getting. "Lead?"

He began massaging my palms with his thumbs. "Relax, cute stuff, I'm not proposing. I like you a lot, and I want to be with you. You're my favorite enigma."

I smiled a little, "Your what?"

"You're outgoing and fun, and yet there is a deep insecurity inside you that's holding you back. I'm intrigued." His expression became more serious. "And if I can I'd like to help."

"Why would you want to help me?"

"Like I said, you fascinate me."

I studied his face. There was definitely something he was holding back. "Hunter, what's going on in that stubborn head of yours?"

He looked at our joined hands for a moment before he raised his head again. "Okay, sweetheart, you asked for it. The truth is, I'm pretty sure I'm falling in love with you."

Chapter Ten

Hunter had to go out of town the next day, which was definitely good for my sanity. I struggled through my morning writing session, the words coming so slowly I felt like my brain was stuck in quicksand. I was not quite at half my usual word count when I decided I'd sat at my desk as long as I could tolerate it. I needed time and space to think as much as I needed air to breathe.

I closed down my laptop and headed toward the kitchen. There I shifted, dove through the doggie door, and ran around the yard as hard and fast as my canine legs would take me.

Eventually I needed to take a break, and lying in the soft grass near the back door, I let the sun warm my belly, while my stupid human mind bounced around like a kitten playing with a new toy.

Hunter and I had agreed to see each other exclusively, which was hardly a big deal for me. It wasn't like men were knocking down my door or anything. I dated sometimes, but mostly I stayed to myself and didn't think much about it. When you're a shapeshifter, dating comes with issues that I didn't want to face. I'd freaked over seeing my own father shift, shifting in front of a guy I cared about was the kind of thing that provoked nightmares.

And yeah, I cared about Hunter more than I really

83

wanted to admit, even to myself. The last thing I wanted was to traumatize the man. He didn't even believe in Bigfoot or leprechauns or faeries—and he'd seen examples of all three of them. Forcing him to believe by seeing his girlfriend shift probably wouldn't be good.

Just to confuse things even more, a part of me wondered where he'd had to go right after agreeing to be exclusive. To break up with his last exclusive woman?

Ugh, I didn't like the formal sound of that. Saying you're "exclusive" is about as romantic as saying you have a dental appointment. "We're going steady" is probably not a term adult-type people use, but I liked it better. I didn't even think it was still a high school expression, not that I learned much about dating and such in high school. That pesky shapeshifting thing interfered in everything because I was constantly afraid somebody would find out I was not like everybody else. It was one more teenage problem on top of all the usual stuff. Like high school isn't hard enough.

I got up and shot around the yard like I was running from something. Probably my life.

It took probably another hour to wear myself out enough to head back into the house. After a shower and a huge turkey, beef, and bologna sandwich, I curled up on the couch to read the newest celebrity magazine. I was relaxed and bordering on nap mode when a knock on my door interrupted. Hoping it was something interesting, but figuring it was Miz Carlisle come to complain, I pulled the door.

And stood staring, with my mouth open.

I couldn't believe he'd actually come to *my* house.

Well, Aunt Ruth's house—where I was living at the moment. But there he was, standing outside my front door. Anger filled my chest and sounded clearly in my voice. "What do you want?"

"Have you seen her?"

"Have I seen who?"

"Rose."

I shook my head in an effort to shift the pieces of my brain back into place. "I don't know a Rose."

"She's only fourteen and she's trying to find you."

I saw Miz Carlisle peeking through her germaniums and stepped back. "Come inside."

Once the door was closed I turned to my dad. "Why is a fourteen-year-old girl trying to find me?"

He closed his eyes for a moment, then met my gaze. "Because she's your sister."

All the pain, disappointment, grief, and guilt suddenly boiled over inside me, spewing hot fury through my body. "How dare you come here asking me about a sister I didn't know I had, when you left me when I was four?" I poked him in the chest. "I needed you, you bastard. Mom needed you too. But you weren't there. And you tell me there's a sister I've never even heard about? Why should I even believe you?"

"Because it's true."

"Bull chips."

"Look you can believe whatever you want about me, but there is a scared, confused, angry little girl out there. She's convinced she has to find you."

"Why would she think that?"

"I haven't the foggiest."

I opened my mouth to chew him out, but when I

looked into his eyes, I saw sadness and pain that even my rage at his betrayal couldn't ignore. "I really have a sister?"

"Yes, you do." He pulled out his wallet and showed me the photo of a long-legged, skinny girl who looked a lot like me.

Pain bit into my heart and twisted. "You told her about me."

"No."

My gaze jerked up to look at him. "You just said she was looking for me."

"But I didn't tell her. I wanted to, but it didn't seem right for her to know about you when I didn't think you knew about her."

"You didn't *think* I knew? How the bloody hell would I have known?"

"You mom didn't want you to know, but I thought she might have told you at some point."

His words turned the pain into anger and blew my emotional control to shreds. "My mother! Oh, so Mom is responsible for all your problems? What kind of man are you? How dare you come here after all these years and try to pretend you're some sort of victim of my mom's decisions. When you know damn well she's not around to defend herself."

"I'm responsible for my own problems. I would have respected Becky's wishes and stayed away, but Rose's actions forced my hand."

"You couldn't have contacted me? Not once in all this time have you even tried, and now you're blaming my mother and my sister? What a jerk!" I turned my back because I damn well didn't want him to see me cry.

"I'm not blaming anybody, Terri. All I'm saying is that I'm worried about Rose."

"You never worried about me!"

"I did worry about you."

I spun to face him, and he held out a hand to stop me. "I get that you don't believe me, and I don't blame you. If you want to beat the hell out of me later, I won't stop you. Right now, though, there's a fourteen-year-old who needs our help."

What else could I do? "Fine. I'll keep an eye out for her."

"Thank you, Terri." With that he turned and left, closing the door behind him.

It took me a moment to get myself pulled together enough to think. Only then did it occur to me to ask how he knew she was looking for me. And if she was a shifter. I threw open the door and rushed out onto the porch, but the only thing I saw was a blue car turning onto the main road. I didn't even know if it was his car. So I went back inside and sprawled on the couch. I had a freaking sister. A fourteen-year-old sister. I couldn't help myself, I grinned.

****

I was in my Trixie form and doing laps in the yard, my favorite way to think—and, until recently, a guaranteed way to bust writers block. Right now though, I was trying to figure out what the bloody hell my dad wanted with me after twenty-five years. He said he needed my help. With my little sister. What kind of crazy was that?

I caught a glimpse of movement across the road, and slid to a stop near the front gate. It was an animal, for sure, and my nose told me it was canine. There was something about the scent that seemed familiar, and I was thinking about jumping the fence to go check it out when the dog moved fully into my vision.

A collie. A rough collie, like the fictional Lassie. Like me.

She moved a little closer and I saw she was a puppy. Not a little one, but not totally grown either. The girl was beautiful, and I felt a strong need to go over there, but she was skittish, and I didn't want to frighten her. I told her I wouldn't hurt her, but she backed up, then turned and ran away.

I stood there for a minute, head tilted, wondering where that dog had come from. I'd never seen her before, but somebody could have just adopted her. She didn't have a collar, but maybe she'd slipped out of it, or the humans hadn't got one for her yet.

I started toward the back. Bumpkins and Scrappy were playing, and joining them might take my mind off things. I was almost there when it hit me. The scent I'd picked up from the new dog but hadn't been able to place. It was human, and not just where a person had touched her. This scent was embedded in her own.

Was it possible the dog I'd seen was a shifter?

Leaving the cats to play, I went into the house where I could be alone. My heart was twisting and my head was pounding. Hunter, my dad, the possibility that things weren't as I'd always believed them. That I'd seen a shifter across the road. A shifter that looked like me, smelled like me.

That might well be my sister?

Chapter Eleven

Over the next few hours I worked myself up into a crying jag, an eat-dirt-and-die depression, and anger so thick I could probably chew it up for fun. I paced, I cried, I paced some more, I cried again. I shifted and ran around outside for a while. I changed back, got dressed just in case somebody came by, slept for a whole twenty minutes, then went through the pacing and crying cycle again. I was exhausted and shaky, but still I wasn't sure how I felt about my dad, my sister, or even my mom.

The sound of footsteps shot several emotions through me one after the other. I hoped it was Shay, but a glance out the window sent a whole new set of emotions through me. I pulled the door open before Hunter could knock. He took one look at me, his eyes widened, and he pulled me into his arms, shoving the door closed behind him with one foot.

"What happened?"

I snuggled against his warm, strong chest. "My dad stopped by."

"What did he do that upset you so badly?"

"He said I have a sister and she's looking for me. But he said she didn't know about me, which makes no sense. But she's fourteen, and she's my sister, and I had to say I would watch for her, but why didn't he tell me before? And he said my mom knew about my sister. He said they'd been talking, but she never said anything to me. What the hell is going on?"

Somehow we'd wound up on the couch. Hunter was holding me close and rubbing my back. "Oh, honey. I'm so sorry. Is there anything I can do to make you feel better?"

"I don't know. I'm so confused."

"I know you are. That's a lot to take in at one time, and from a man you haven't seen in years. Did something happen back then, or did he just leave? Do you know?"

I opened my mouth to tell him what happened, but even in my ragged emotional state, I managed to catch myself before I said something I would definitely regret. "I remember Mom and Dad fighting, but I don't know what they were fighting about."

"He just showed up and said you have a sister?"

"He said she's looking for me." I looked into Hunter's sweet, caring eyes. "But he said she didn't know she had a sister because Mom didn't want me to know about her. It doesn't make sense."

"It really doesn't." He kissed my forehead. "You're shaking, Terri. Have you had anything to eat recently?"

I thought about it. "I know I had breakfast." Sheesh, I don't forget to eat. Ever. Shifting takes a lot of energy, so I tend to consume a lot.

"Let's find you something to get your blood sugar out of the basement."

I leaned against his firm, warm body as we walked into the kitchen. He deposited me in a chair at the table and opened the fridge. "Is this lasagna?"

My stomach woke up. "Yeah, I made it yesterday. It just needs to be heated up."

He warmed the food and sat a plate in front of me. "Eat," he said, as he took the chair next to me with a serving of his own.

Within a few minutes, my stomach was happy, the shaking had stopped, and I felt strength returning. "Thank you, Hunter."

"For what?"

I gave a one-shouldered shrug. "Listening, feeding me, being so sweet."

He smiled softly. "That's what people do when they care deeply about someone else."

I took his hand in mine and let my gaze remain where they joined. "I haven't had a lot of experience with that kind of thing."

"There's my enigma girl again." He smiled gently. "You're energetic, outgoing, a lot of fun; but you also seem almost naive at times. Like you've spent a lot of time alone."

I forced a little laugh. "I'm a writer, of course I've spent a lot of time alone."

"Not exactly what I'm talking about."

"You're confusing me." I smiled to cover my discomfort.

"I'm worried about you."

My confusion shot up a few more points. "What are you talking about?"

He gently squeezed my hand as he leaned toward me. "Sweetheart, were you abused?"

I knocked the chair over as I jumped to my feet and backed up a step. "No! Why would you even think that? My mom is wonderful. I can't believe you'd say something like that. That's horrible!"

Hunter stood slowly, holding up his hands in

surrender. "Honey, something is not adding up. Your mom is great, I get that, but maybe a neighbor, uncle, teacher. Your father. Maybe somebody scared you, hurt you."

The fear in his expression reminded me of my mom when I'd run to her after dad shifted in front of me. When he scared me so badly it had taken a long time not to be afraid of my own kind. Well, half-kind.

I shook my head to clear my thoughts. Daddy scaring me wasn't the problem. I was isolated growing up, still am. I have to be careful what I say to people, what I do. And if I don't shift for a while, I start feeling all twitchy and weird.

"Terri? Are you all right?"

I wasn't abused. I knew what the issue was. All I had to do was tell him. It was my story to tell. I wouldn't be telling anybody else's secret, only mine. He probably wouldn't believe it, but I could prove it pretty easily. And then what? Hunter had his own issues. He was not likely to easily accept what I am. If he did accept me, his world would be changed in a way that he might not be happy about.

Either way, there was a good chance I'd lose him forever.

"Terri," he said again."

"I'm all right, Hunter." I shoved my gaze up to meet his. "I wasn't abused. Honest. There are things I'm not ready to talk about. Could you give me a little time, please?"

He moved closer so he could pull me into his arms. "I'll give you whatever you need. Just please promise me you'll tell me if there is anything I can do to help or make you feel better." He stepped back so he could look me in the eye. "Promise?"

"Promise."

His lips touched mine, and a tingling sensation moved through my body. I'm not totally naive, I knew what was happening. I just couldn't think. I probably should stop this, but I really didn't want to. I never wanted to leave Hunter's arms. I never wanted him to stop kissing me. I never wanted his hand to stop roaming over my back and neck.

His hand slipped under my T-shirt and travelled up to the side of my breast. I moaned, and he chuckled.

"Like this, do you?"

"Yes!"

He shifted his hand so it enveloped my breast, then moved enough to tease my bra-covered nipple. For a moment I thought I would launch off the kitchen chair. I moaned again, and he responded by moving his hand downward, between my legs, setting me on fire right through the denim of my jeans. He nuzzled my neck, and I gasped for breath.

I got hold of his shirt and worked at remembering how to unbutton. All I could think was how warm and firm the muscles under his shirt felt. He unsnapped my jeans, and had just got hold of the zipper when I heard the front door open.

We jerked apart like we'd been shocked. I snapped my pants, and we were straightening our clothes when Shay and Ace rounded the corner into the kitchen.

"Hunter, hey."

Hunter stood, and the two men did the whole hand-shaking, back-slapping, sort-of-hugging thing that guys do.

Meanwhile, Shay regarded me with one raised

eyebrow. "I need to get some stuff from my bedroom. Terri, why don't you help me?"

She grabbed my arm, and we headed past the guys. Hunter looked at me and cringed. I gave him what I hoped was an it's-fine smile, but I figured it was more like an I'm-screwed one.

Shay closed the door and crossed her arms. "Okay, spill. I want details, Cuz."

"My dad called a couple of days ago."

Shay stopped in mid step. "That's seriously weird, and I want to hear all about it. But what I want to know right now is why you and Hunter Devereux were making out in our kitchen? That is Hunter Devereux, right?"

"Yes, that's Hunter." I took a deep breath and dove in. "Dad came by here earlier today. He says I have a sister named Rose, she's fourteen and she's looking for me. Oh, and by the way, he and Mom have kept in touch all these years, and she was the one who didn't want him to contact me. He says she knew about my sister too, but didn't want me to know she existed."

"Holy dysfunctional family."

"When Hunter came by I was still upset, so he comforted me."

"By making out with you in the kitchen."

"He was so sweet. He listened, he made me laugh, he reminded me to eat. He held me and kissed me, and…"

"Named you George?"

I groaned, but didn't hit her. "Ha-ha."

"Sorry. So you're saying nature took its course."

I sat on the edge of her bed. "I don't know much about nature, and men, and stuff."

"Stuff? As in sex?"

I couldn't speak, so I nodded.

She sat beside me and wrapped an arm around my shoulders. "Ah, sweetie. I think I get why you're so uncomfortable. You really haven't done a lot of socializing, especially with boys."

"I had to be so careful." I thought about all the lonely days when I claimed to have things to do, while everyone I knew was out having a good time.

"Not a lot of room for boyfriends."

I closed my eyes and let my head fall forward. "One."

"Did you say one?"

"Yes."

"As in one boyfriend?"

"Yes."

Shay blew out breath. "We're pathetic."

I looked at her. "How many have you had?"

There was a pause, and I wondered if she was going to answer. "Four, not including Ace. He's special."

Her dreamy expression made me smile. "So, have you set a date yet?"

"No. We're still discussing details."

I smiled. She looked so happy. "Well get on it, girl. I can't wait to be your..." Then I realized, she hadn't asked. "Um, to be your helper getting things together."

She nodded. "Good, because bridesmaids are supposed to assist the bride. Lord knows, I certainly need help."

She hugged me, then stood. "But first, I need to go introduce myself to somebody."

I was caught for a moment in thoughts of my sweet

cousin getting married, with a side trip into the fantasy-land of me in a beautiful white dress. And Hunter in a tux. Hunter!

I trucked into the living room, where I heard Hunter say, "It's nice to meet you, Shay."

She sat on the couch near him and they shook hands, but instead of letting go of his hand she leaned closer. "If you do anything that hurts my cousin, I'll tear your face off and feed it to my dog."

She let go then and walked away. Hunter, who had gone pale, glanced toward his friend.

"Don't look at me," Ace said. "I'd help her."

I grabbed Shay's arm as she passed me on the way back to her bedroom. "What was that?"

She smiled. "I love you, Terri. You're the sister I never had. Being able to scare the bow tie off tall and nerdy over there for you was one of the most amazing moments of my life."

"Thanks," I whispered.

"Anytime." She gave me a hug. "Now, I really do have stuff I need to get together to take back to Ace's."

"You're going back to his house?" I felt a little twinge of guilt about being glad.

Her smile was borderline evil. "That way, we both have privacy to do whatever we want."

She went into the bedroom, and I headed toward the living room. Hunter saw me and smiled, and tingles shot from my head to my toes. I sat beside him, and he took my hand in his. "I like your cousin."

I looked at him, wondering how that worked. "She threatened you, but you like her?"

He brushed a stray lock of hair off my face. "When you care about a person you want to protect them."

"You wouldn't hurt me."

"She doesn't know that." He touched his index finger to my nose. "And, though I appreciate your faith in me, neither do you. Not really."

For reasons I didn't want to look at too closely, tears stung my eyes. "But you wouldn't."

He pressed his palm against my cheek. "No, sweetheart. I'd never hurt you, and I'd kill anybody who did. I'm just pointing out another indication of that innocent, trusting nature. Odd for a woman who's had so much heartache."

"Not so much."

His lips became a straight line and he shook his head just a little. "Honey…"

I shot a glance toward the bedroom where Ace had joined my cousin. "Shay's dad died when she wasn't even a teenager, then her mother got really depressed and Shay had to take care of her. This last year was the first time since she was a kid that she could focus on her own life." I held his gaze. "That's heartache."

He glanced toward Shay's bedroom and nodded. "She had a rough time, for sure." His fingertip brushed gently across my lips. "Which does nothing to lessen the pain you've endured in your life."

"I have a feeling you've had a rough life too."

"Again, doesn't diminish your own pain."

I lowered my gaze, not sure what to say or do.

"Hey, I didn't mean to upset you."

"You didn't." I managed a little smile. "I'm just don't see myself as somebody who's been hurt that much."

"Maybe that's why you're still a trusting person."

"I think it's more like I can sense who to trust and

who not to."

He studied my face for a moment, then grinned. "I don't buy it. You trust me, don't you?"

"Mostly."

"Mostly, huh?"

I nodded, but further conversation was postponed by the two returning to the living room. "We're heading back to Ace's house," Shay said as she scratched Scrappy's head and back. "Call if you need anything."

"Yeah, like throwing the trash out." Ace made a vague gesture toward Hunter.

"Watch it Ellison," Hunter said.

"You don't scare me, bow tie man."

"That's enough boys," Shay said. She gave me a hug. The men shook hands, and I hugged Ace before the two of them headed out.

I locked the door behind them, and I was left again with the man who I wasn't sure what to do with. We sat on the couch, and Hunter smiled softly as he brushed a stray bit of hair behind my shoulder. "I can't believe your cousin is engaged to Ace Ellison."

"I'm amazed you two know each other."

He shrugged. "Small world."

"Apparently so."

Scrappy seemed to realize they weren't coming back and jumped into a chair. She curled up and immediately went to sleep.

"What did Ace tell you about me?" Hunter asked.

"Not a lot. Just that you worked together in South America."

"That was a really amazing trip. Ace and I had a lot of fun."

I giggled. I couldn't help it. The picture in my head

was just too funny

"Why are you laughing?"

"The thought of the two of you together. There isn't video, is there? I would pay good money to see that."

Hunter narrowed his eyes. "What else did he tell you?"

"He said he hid your fez." The idea of Hunter wearing a fez was so cute and silly at the same time that I started laughing again.

"So he admitted to that, did he?" I nodded, and Hunter shook his head. "That guy is a something else."

"He's a lot of fun."

"You like him, huh?"

"Yeah, I do."

Hunter's eyes went dark. "Should I be jealous?"

"No," I whispered.

He leaned in and captured my mouth. Without a second thought I reached around his neck and pulled him closer. He teased my lips, and my mouth relaxed to let him in. His tongue caressed mine, and my heart skipped a beat, then another. I moaned and tightened my arms around him.

He slid his hands up and down my back as if he were trying to touch my soul with his fingertips. Then one hand cupped my butt and pulled me closer. The other hand slipped under my shirt and up to caress my breast.

I sighed and he buried his face in my neck, trailing kisses up and down from my jaw to my collarbone.

"I want you so much it hurts," he whispered.

All ten of my fingers grabbed hold of his shirt fabric and hung on. "Hunter."

He snuggled me even closer. "Ah, Terri. You are the sexiest woman I've ever met."

I wanted to laugh. Or cry. Not sure which. What I did was force my fingers loose of his shirt. "There's a lot you don't know about me."

"We'll get to know each other slowly. There's no need to rush anything, including this." He gave me a wobbly smile.

I blinked back tears as I flattened my palms against his chest and gave him a pathetic shove. "There's something you need to know." I met his gaze with my own. "Something I need you to know."

"What is it, sweetheart?"

I was pretty sure I was going to choke on my own tears. "I haven't had a lot of experience."

"Sexual experience?"

I nodded. "I stayed to myself most of the time. I don't have many friends, and I don't get out much."

"We writers are not known for being social."

"Well, I may hold the record when it comes to relationships." My face went hot, and I lowered my head to hide it.

Hunter ran a gentle fingertip down my cheek. "Terri, are you saying you're a virgin?"

I was surprised I didn't literally die of humiliation, but I managed to nod.

Chapter Twelve

"You have nothing to be ashamed of."

"Right." I shoved myself to my feet and went over to the window so I could breathe. Across the way, I could see Miz C. in her flower garden. "I'm a perfectly normal woman who's a year and two weeks away from being the embodiment of the 'thirty year-old virgin' joke."

"Your birthday's in two weeks?"

"Yeah. My twenty-ninth." I sighed.

"So, are you planning on having friends come up from Florida or maybe going to Jacksonville for a couple of days, or—"

"I really hadn't thought about it."

"Hadn't thought about it? And it's your twenty-ninth too! What do you normally do on your birthday?"

I shrugged. "Mom and I go out for dinner and she gets a cake from the bakery. Diara and I try to go shopping or something."

"Diara?"

"My best friend." I swallowed back the pain that abruptly filled my chest. I hadn't realized how much I missed her until now.

"Maybe she can come up for the big event. I'm sure Shay, and Ace, will want to do something for you. How big a celebration would you prefer?"

I was staring at him. Hard stare. But he didn't seem

to realize how freaked out I was. "Hunter?"

He looked at me, and was on his feet in seconds, hurrying over to me. "Did I do something wrong, honey?"

I looked down. "It's odd having somebody excited about my birthday."

"I can't believe you don't enjoy your birthdays more."

"I didn't say I don't enjoy my birthdays. I just don't do big parties or stuff."

"Any particular reason?" He planted a quick kiss on the tip of my nose. "You don't seem shy."

I half-watched Miz C as she tried to pretend she wasn't spying when it was obvious she was. "Mom and I live on an old farm in the boonies. Living there is awesome, but being so far out makes it hard to socialize."

"You don't like that part."

Damn the man. "It's okay. I tend to keep to myself most of the time anyway."

He cupped my chin and tipped it up. "When you're ready to talk about the rest of the story, I'll be there to listen."

Tears stung my eyes. "Thank you, Hunter."

He smiled as he leaned down to touch his lips to mine. The kiss sent heat blazing through me, into the most vulnerable, intimate pats of my body. His hand slid down to cup my rear and tug me closer. I felt him then, the hard expression of his desire for me. My body moved against him, craving what only he could give.

He groaned against my hair. "You make me crazy, Terri Quinn."

"I want you," I whispered.

He looked at me, studying my face. "Honey, please be sure. If you need me to stop I will, but I think it might kill me."

"I'm sure."

He looked at me for a moment, then grinned and literally swept me off my feet. He took me into my bedroom and sat me back on my feet near the bed. Seconds later my T-shirt was flying in the general direction of a chair near the corner of the room.

With shaking hands, I pulled the bottom of Hunter's shirt out of his pants and he helped me get it off of him. The sight of his chest had my breath catching in my throat. Dark hair covered a wall of muscle. I pressed my palms against him. Warm and firm. Amazing.

I felt him touch my back just before my bra popped loose. He moved my hands from his chest one at a time so he could slide off my bra. Then he just looked at me for a moment.

"Something wrong?"

"Not a damn thing." He put his hand on one breast and leaned in to take the other nipple into his mouth.

I moaned so hard it was almost a scream, and I think I'd have collapsed if he hadn't put an arm around me and held me up. After a time he switched and took the other nipple in his mouth.

"Sweet," he whispered.

I realized my jeans were unfastened when I felt them being tugged down my legs. "Hunter!" It was half-word half-gasp.

He lowered me to the bed, divested himself of the rest of his clothes, and then he very slowly slipped my panties down my legs. I watched his face as he looked

Cheryel Hutton

at me, and I felt little dances inside me just from his expression. Then he edged my legs apart and slid one hand up my thigh to gently brush my most intimate area. I gasped as my back arched.

He kissed me long and thoroughly, while his fingers continued to explore. I wrapped my arms around his neck and hug on. His touch had me all but crazy when he slipped a finger inside me. I felt his long, warm body press against my side. It was an amazing feeling that made me want to run my hands all over him. I couldn't though, both from shyness and from the intensity of the feelings he was evoking inside me.

He ran a line of kisses down to my breasts where he proceeded to spark some even more amazing sensations. Meanwhile he inserted more fingers inside. Preparing me, I supposed. I really couldn't think very well.

He moved away, and I grabbed at him. "Just a second, honey. I promise."

He tore open a small package and rolled a condom onto a part of him that suddenly looked huge. He looked at me and grinned. "Are you impressed or terrified?"

"Both," I managed.

"I won't hurt you." He kissed me gently while his hand went back to doing wonderful things to first my breasts and then down and between my legs again. He edged my legs wide and knelt between them. "Relax," he whispered. "Look at me, sweetheart."

I looked into his eyes, and I felt him at my entrance. "It's going to be all right," he said. He lowered his head and nipped my earlobe.

The nip startled me, but it didn't really hurt. It did

distract me for a moment, easing the shock of his body moving into mine. I bit my lip to keep from crying out. "Sorry, honey," he whispered.

The pain quickly subsided, and something else took its place. My hips moved, and I wanted him to touch me again.

He kissed me, then licked my nipples while he reached between us and touched me. It still hurt a little when he started moving, but I was so caught up in the moment I barely noticed. Hunter went still and I knew he was there. I knew enough to know that was likely the end of the experience. But he surprised me by taking a nipple in his mouth just as he used his fingers to gently touch me in my most sensitive spot. Heat gathered inside me so fast I grabbed his shoulders to steady myself.

"Hunter," I gasped.

"Your turn," he said, then looked me straight in the eye as he sucked at first one nipple, then another. Slowly he increased the intensity of his stroking, and it didn't take much more for me to have an orgasm so intense I wasn't sure it would ever stop. Then he collapsed beside me.

A few minutes later, he moved away and cleaned himself up while I went to the bathroom and did the same. Back in the bedroom, we lay together on the bed and simply held on to each other.

I know a lot of people think the first time isn't a big deal. For me it was huge. For better or worse, I knew my world would never be the same again.

Chapter Thirteen

The brightness of the rising sun's rays pulled me from sleep. It was an odd sensation, since I was always up long before sunrise. I rolled to my side, and immediately realized three things: one, I was naked; two, I was alone in bed except for a cat; three, Scrappy was staring at me with her big green eyes.

"Are you telling me I should get up and feed you?"

She meowed softly, and I gave her head a scratch. "Give me a minute, furry butt, let me get dressed."

Scrappy didn't seem especially happy with that, but I think she realized there wasn't much she could do about it. I slid out of bed and grabbed fresh clothes. Smells of cooking bacon and eggs came from the kitchen and got me moving. There was also the smell of coffee, but I could ignore that. Did I mention bacon and eggs?

It only took me about five minutes for me to shower, brush my teeth, and prepare my outward self to see Hunter. My inner self was cringing in a corner and saying it was never going to be ready to face the man. What did I know about mornings after? Nothing, that's what.

I cleaned up the bathroom, swallowed my trepidation, and headed toward the kitchen. Hunter looked at me and smiled. "Hope you like a big breakfast.

"I do, and that smells wonderful." I fed Scrappy, got a mug and my tea bags out, and put the kettle on to heat.

"I didn't think you liked coffee, but I wasn't sure if you drank tea for breakfast, or how you fix it."

"No problem." I sighed. "I can't believe I slept so late. I'm usually up writing way before daylight."

He moved so he was standing right beside me. "I wore you out."

My face went hot, and I poked at a tiny spot on the counter. "True."

His hand caressed my back. "Are you okay, sweetheart? I'm sorry I hurt you."

"You didn't." I shrugged. "Well, you did, but not much. Besides, everything else felt so good I barely noticed."

"Next time, after you heal, it'll be better."

I smiled into his gorgeous eyes. "I'm not sure I could handle better."

His big, bright smile warmed my heart. This was a special man, and I knew enough to understand how lucky I was. I got my tea, and carefully sat at the kitchen table. Odd I never realized how hard those chairs were. "This looks delicious. Thank you for cooking."

"I enjoy cooking. I'm not great at it, but I enjoy it."

We ate quietly, and cleaned the kitchen together. Then Hunter faced me and put his hands on my shoulders. "I know you write in the morning, and I have a lot to do also. I'm going back to the B&B for a while."

"Okay," I whispered, not wanting to be obvious that I wanted him to stay.

He kissed my forehead. "If I stick around too much longer, I'm going to forget my vow to give you time to heal, and do something that I won't be happy with myself for doing. How about after we get our work done, I gather my notes and we can discuss your bestseller problem."

My stomach curled up in a ball and hid behind my liver. "It really isn't horrible, right?"

"Not even a little bit." He gave me a soft kiss and headed out. I watched until his car went around the corner and then I went in the kitchen, stripped, shifted, and headed outside.

I ran harder than I had in years. Dogs are more instinctual and less tied to thinking than humans, and I hoped to use that difference to help me get some perspective. I guess it helped, some. But later, as I sat at my laptop trying to figure out if the scene I was writing was pretty good, or the worst piece of literary cow chips ever, I wondered if it was even possible to get perspective on the consequences of the night before. I had serious doubts. My life had changed in a big way.

I finally decided that the only way to manage any kind of perspective would be from somebody outside the situation, so I grabbed my cell phone.

"Well, hello Terri," my best friend Diara said. "I haven't heard from you in a while. Did the Bigfoot tribe bring you back? I knew they wouldn't keep you."

I laughed. "I think I scared the poor things. How's it going down in Jacksonville?"

"Going fairly well except for the wedding thing."

"I thought you said Finley had everything under control."

Diara groaned. "Logistics aren't the problem. The

problem is that the groom is not exactly who she thinks he is."

"As in, he's not really a lawyer from Mississippi?"

"He is that. It's his morals that I'm questioning. I've…um…I've seen visions of him in bed with a woman who definitely isn't my sister."

My breath sucked in hard. "That's not good. Any chance it could be somebody he used to know, who's out of his life now?"

"No way. Whatever is going on with him and her, it's happening now."

"Wow. Have you talked to Finley?"

"I tried. She is totally convinced Scott is the best thing since bagged chips."

I knew what the answer would be, but I asked anyway. "Even though you had a vision?"

"She still thinks psychic phenomenon are bull-crap, and I'm loco for even believing in an ability. No way does she think I could be able to do something so wild and crazy."

"After all these years." I sighed and leaned back against my desk chair. "Good grief."

"What can I say, my sister is stubborn, and Mom's attitude doesn't help any. I'm going to have to figure out how hard to push, I don't want my sister to get hurt, but I don't want to alienate her either."

"Good luck."

"Thanks. So, what's going on with you? And don't tell me nothing is wrong, because I know there is."

I groaned. "This is what happens when your best friend is a psychic."

"Actually it's your voice that gave you away. If I'd had a vision I would have known already. "Spill it,

Quinn. Tell me what's wrong."

"I wouldn't say wrong exactly, just weird."

"What's the guy's name?"

"I didn't say it was a guy."

"I've got news for you. When a woman has issues, especially weird ones, it usually involves a man."

I sighed and gave her points for saying what she thought straight out. "You're right about that, and you're right about me too. He's a writer who's doing a book about Ugly Creek history."

"He's a writer, then you two should understand each other."

"Not so much," I wandered over to the kitchen window and looked out at trees marking the end of Aunt Ruth's property on the cul-de-sac side. "He's a professor type who doesn't think much of books by and for woman."

"Insulting you and Shay in one dislike. But there must be something about the guy you like, or you wouldn't be stressing over him."

There was a girl halfway behind one tree, I couldn't see much of her, but I did see enough to make me wonder.

"Terri?"

I shook away the curiosity. The girl was probably a neighbor kid. "He apologized for the remark. Then he was really nice to me when my dad showed up out of the blue."

"Your dad is there?"

"Somewhere, I guess. He called, which was weird enough, then he just flipping showed up at my door. Said he and Mom have been in touch all this time. She's in a jungle somewhere, so I can't talk to her for a few more days."

"And this guy was there for you?"

"Yeah. He was really sweet. But then, last night things got a little out of hand."

"What are you saying, out of hand?"

"Okay not out of hand exactly. More like…well…intimate."

"Terry Quinn, are you trying to tell me that you and this dude did something that I'll want to hear all the minute details about?"

"Yes. And no, you don't get the details."

"Ah Terri, come on. I have to live vicariously through somebody and it sure as hell is not my sister."

"Sorry about that, but that doesn't mean it's going to be me."

"Oh, come on! Give me something. Who is this guy who's got you all riled up?"

"His name is Hunter and 'riled up' is about the size of it."

I heard a familiar vehicle and smiled. "Speaking of Hunter, he just pulled in. I'll call you tomorrow."

"Promise?"

"I might even give you a few details."

"I'm counting on you."

I hung up, checked my hair and makeup, and headed out the front door to meet the reason for my confusion, the varmint.

I couldn't wait to see him.

****

Hunter met me with a warm kiss and wrapped his arm around me as we walked into the house. Miz C and Bumpkins were near the fence, as always. The cat watched us curiously, and the old woman gave us the evil eye.

Once inside, we got glasses of iced tea and sat on the couch. I was so nervous I almost spilled my tea, and it didn't help that I could smell anxiety on Hunter. What did he plan to tell me that worried him so much?

"First, complete disclosure." He handed me a paperback, a fantasy novel written by one Devon Hunt.

I'd heard the name, but of course I'd had no idea who the author actually was. I turned it over in my hand, examining the shine and wondering what to say. "Yours?"

He nodded. "Look, I'm sure my buddy Ace told you I write commercial fiction. Which makes me a hypocrite, I know."

I smiled as I skimmed the back of the book. "So this is you being a hypocrite? Looks interesting."

"Feel free to read it and tell me what you think. It's only fair." He shrugged. "In fact, if you get really crazy, I have three more. Just let me know."

With that, the itchy feeling I'd had all morning kicked up a good ten notches. "About my books…"

He took my hand in his. "You're an excellent writer. Technique is not your problem."

"Then what is?"

He met my gaze, and the expression I saw in his eyes shifted. He didn't want to tell me. My breath got so choppy it made me feel funny. "Terri?" He touched my face. "It's not that bad. I'm just not sure how to explain what I think."

"Try, please."

He nodded. "In your early books, you went deep. You tapped into your heart, your passion, your soul."

My mouth went dry. "Not now?"

He took a breath. "Your books are well plotted, and the characters are interesting, but it feels like the stories are coming from here." He touched a fingertip to my forehead. "Not here." He touched my breastbone.

I wanted to laugh, to tell him he was full of something stinky. A tiny part of me, though, whispered I'd known all along. A bucket of cold fear poured over me. "So I lost my writing mojo."

Hunter's soft chuckle warmed me and irritated me at the same time. "No," he said. "In my opinion, you have lost your excitement for writing women's fiction. It seems to me that you're forcing the story to come. Maybe you need to try a different type of story or genre. Writing is hard enough without forcing yourself to write something you dislike."

I looked at him, and saw the face of a professor. A person who made his living putting fiction into pigeonholes. "So, give my muse something different to work with?"

He shrugged. "You could put it like that."

"But you wouldn't." I stood and went into the kitchen. I looked out the window above the sink, but I didn't see the teenage girl. Why did that bother me?

Hunter's hand rested on my shoulder. "I was afraid I would upset you. I'm sorry."

It was all too much. A sister I didn't know. A father I barely remembered. A career I loved, and needed to survive in the crazy human world, was threatened by my own inability to know what I wanted to do. Tears abruptly filled my eyes, which irritated the last nerve standing.

"Wouldn't do to believe in a muse, would it? That's entirely too much like fun. Might not take the magic out of writing. You don't want to believe in anything you can't measure or calculate somehow. You can't let yourself believe in muses, or Bigfoot, or ghosts, or shapeshifters. I'm amazed you can write fiction at all, much less fantasy."

Dead silence closed around us, closing off even the quiet movement of the air as we breathed. A dull ache filled my chest as I considered the possibility that I'd just done the irreparable.

"That's not fair, Terri."

"Life's not fair." The words were out of my mouth before I made the decision to speak.

"I see life through the eyes of science and logic," he said. "I don't believe in what I can't verify. You believe in things I don't. The differences in how we see the world allows me to write fantasy; and for you to write best-selling women's fiction. The world would be boring if we all saw things the same way."

I looked at him through a new batch of tears. "I'm sorry."

"You've had a rough time the last few days."

I held his gaze. "It *is* magic, you know. We have the ability to visit a non-existent world and write down the stories we encounter there so that other people can visit that world too."

Hunter looked thoughtful for a moment, then a smile lit his face. "I really like that."

"Even if you don't believe—" Hunter touched the tip of his finger to my lips.

"Just because I understand how the process works doesn't mean I can't see the magic in what we do."

I narrowed my eyes. "Nobody understands how we manage to make stories in our heads and transfer them to paper. What we do goes way beyond the basic formation of thoughts and imagination, neurons and electrical impulses."

He chuckled. "Okay. Nobody really understands how the mind works when it's being creative, true. But we do know a lot more than we did. Now we know that there are three networks in the brain that work together when we're creative, The Executive Attention Network, The Default Network, and The Salience Network. Plus we know during a creative process our brains activate and deactivate the dorsolateral prefrontal cortex."

I took a tiny step so that our bodies almost touched. "We? So you're a neuroscientist now? Or is there a mouse in your pocket?"

He pulled out his left pants pocket and peered down into it. "She's on to us, Pedro."

I rolled my eyes, but he was so cute it was impossible to be angry. Still that didn't change the fact that if our relationship had any chance of being more than a quick, fun fling, he would have to accept something very non-logical about me.

Hunter's fingers tipped up my chin. "Pedro wants to know why you have that worried look on your face."

It would be easy to go along with the light conversation, but after the last few crazy days, I was in serious need of some hope. So I dove in. "What would it take for you to believe in something paranormal?"

His lips pulled to one side in an expression that was likely exasperation. "What is it with you? Why is it so important to you that I believe in that off-the-wall stuff that you do?"

Because I'm a collie. I sighed. "Please go with me for a minute. What would cause you to rethink your opinion?"

His frown deepened. "It isn't an opinion. I'm simply seeing the world through logic and science."

I held up a hand. "What would it take for you to admit there are things beyond today's scientific knowledge?"

"There are things beyond what we know. I don't question that."

There was my opening, now to take it. "Okay, let's take Bigfoot. Isn't it possible that there is an animal that we don't know about roaming the deep forests?"

He shifted from one leg to another for a moment before he spoke. "I can't believe nobody's found a body or something by now, but I'll give you the benefit of the doubt. It's not at all likely, but yeah, it's possible."

I swallowed hard and took the next step. "What about leprechauns?"

He groaned. "Oh good grief."

I put my hand on his shoulder. "Hunter, please."

He looked into my eyes, and must have seen something that touched him. "I believe there are people who believe they are leprechauns."

"All it would take are a few genetic and cultural differences to move from belief to reality."

He leaned his head slightly to one side, as his eyes unfocused. He was quiet for a moment, then looked at me again. "Maybe."

"Thank you."

He took a step back and did a little bow. "I concede the point to m'lady."

"What about shapeshifters?"

He let out a long, groaning sigh and his head dropped forward. "I don't know what you want from me. It's beginning to seem like you're trying to provoke an argument."

I touched his arm. "I'm not, I promise. Just tell me your thoughts, then you can change the subject to anything you want."

He looked at me as if calculating the probability I would actually let it go.

"I promise," I said.

He sighed again and looked me directly in the eyes. "Shapeshifting is an impossibility. Just the difference in mass makes it impossible. Changing biological material in what, minutes? Seconds? That definitely breaks the laws of physics."

"Thank you. Just remember in the days to come, you admitted there are things science can't explain."

His eyebrows shot up and his head tipped to one side as he studied me. Then he shook his head slightly as a little breath blew through his lips. "Sure."

I wanted to laugh and cry at the same time. I could show him, of course, but I doubted that would increase the odds of our relationship working.

"So," he said. "How would you feel about going to see that new science fiction movie?"

"Sounds great."

As we got into Hunter's car, I caught a glimpse of a collie puppy. I sniffed, and discovered a scent that was both odd and strangely familiar. Was my sister, one of the impossibilities Hunter couldn't believe existed?

Chapter Fourteen

It was early afternoon two days after our near-argument about the paranormal. Hunter was back at the B&B, working diligently on his book, and I was using the time to set up the next stage in what I hoped was a plan that led to better understanding—and eventual acceptance by the man I loved. The only hitch in the plan was the necessity of involving a friend to make a necessary connection. I'd known about the Bigfoot for years, but had never actually met one. It was time I did.

The foliage thickened as we walked deeper into the woods. Beside me, Stephie had her head down and stepped carefully. Poor thing. She'd told me about a run-in with a rattlesnake not long after she came to Ugly Creek. Maybe I should tell her there was nothing to worry about, I was keeping all my Sleuth Dog senses open to any sort of danger. But then I'd have to tell her my secret.

Maybe that's exactly what I should do, tell her. She was trusting me with a bigger secret, after all. A secret that an entire town worked to protect. Since I wasn't opening up to her, she had no way of knowing that I understood the risk she was taking.

"Thank you for doing this, Stephie."

She glanced toward me. "Please don't make me regret it."

The gravity of the situation rushed over me again.

"I won't. I really do have a good reason for talking to him."

I would tell her later. After I managed to get through whatever happened between Hunter and me. After I either convinced him to open his mind, or I lost him for good.

She stopped and held out a hand to hold me back. "Is anyone there?"

Something was there, I smelled the sharp wild scent of a forest dweller. My heart banged in my chest and I had to fight the strong urge to shift and rush to meet the newcomer.

The magnificent creature looked a lot like the costumed creations from TV. This guy was real, though. No doubt about that. There was no faking that rich, thick fur or the muscles in his face. His expressions were as clear and rich as any other living creature.

"Hello, Abukcheech," Stephie said. "This is my friend Terri. She wanted to meet one of your kind."

I held out my hand in Abukcheech's direction. "It's great to meet you."

"Humans touch hands. I have seen." He covered my hand with his huge, furry one, and I fought the urge to giggle.

A moment later, he had let go of my hand, but was still looking at me. His head was tilted to the side, and his eyes were narrowed. All in all a very human expression. "Is something wrong?"

"You different. Smell different."

Stephie let out a tiny, embarrassed laugh. "Um, Abukcheech, that wasn't nice."

"It's okay," I said, as I smiled at him. "Animals

depend more on scent than humans, I get that."

"I not animal."

"I didn't mean to insult you." Though he looked more confused than insulted.

I tried again. "You use your sense of smell a lot, right?"

He touched his nose. "Smell tell you much." He pointed at Stephie. "You have dog smell with you, but you smell like human."

She smiled. "Because I played with Dingo this morning."

He pointed at me. "She smell like dog."

"Abukcheech!" Stephie's eyes were wider than I'd ever seen a person's get, and she was chewing at her bottom lip so intensely I was worried she'd hurt herself. Screw keeping my frigging secret.

"It's okay. He's both literal and correct. I'm a shapeshifter."

"You're a *what*?"

"I guess you'd say I'm a were-dog. Were-collie to be exact."

"I don't understand."

"Let's just say you won't see Trixie and Terri at the same time."

I looked back at Abukcheech. "That's why I need your help. I have a friend who doesn't believe in anything he can't totally understand. I hope that if he sees that the Dyami are real, he'll be more open to other things."

"Like a shapeshifter girlfriend?" Stephie asked.

"Yes." I turned again to Abukcheech. "Will you help me?"

"What must I do?"

"Just meet me here tomorrow. How about the same time as today?"

"I will do that."

They were both looking at me in oddly similar confusion. "Stephie, if you would be so kind as to take my dog and my clothes with you, I'll show you what I'm talking about."

She nodded, so I slipped behind a tree and turned my back to keep the furry kid from accidentally seeing something he shouldn't. Then I allowed my body to flow into my four-legged form.

There was a feminine gasp then a guttural sounding non-English word followed by a similarly guttural "Awesome." I couldn't resist, I went over to them and did a little bow.

Stephie helped me get free of the shorts and T-shirt still hanging off my body, then folded and gathered them and my shoes. Meanwhile, Abukcheech was watching me intently while doing a little dance. He looked a little like a giant Snoopy. When I caught his gaze, he grinned a big, furry grin. "I will be here tomorrow."

I nodded, then Stephie and I took off down the barely noticeable trail we'd come in on. I sincerely hoped I could locate the trail by myself tomorrow. It be rather embarrassing if after all this I screwed up the opportunity by losing my way in the woods. What kind of dog would that make me? I'd be the laughing stock of the human and the canine world simultaneously.

As we headed toward home, I caught a familiar scent. A moment later I saw the collie puppy peering around a tree. She was looking right at me, her head leaned to the side as if she were trying to figure me out.

I started toward her, but I hadn't taken four steps before she turned tail and ran deeper into the forest. All the way to Stephie's car, and even as she drove us home, I wondered if that puppy was my sister. If so, why didn't Daddy tell me she's a shifter? Worse, what if she'd seen me shift and got scared?

So many things I didn't know. So much I wanted to physically pull from my—our—father.

At Aunt Ruth's house I nosed the keys from my shorts pocket toward Stephie, and in minutes we were inside and away from prying neighbor eyes. I headed into my bedroom, where I shifted back and got dressed.

Back in the living room, Stephie was sitting in the middle of the floor, rolling a ball around so Scrappy could chase it. She looked up when I came into the room. "She's so cute!"

I sat near them so I could play too. "She is, isn't she?"

Stephie was giving me odd little glances.

"Wanna tell me what's up?" I asked.

She giggled. "A dog with a kitten pet."

I groaned. "You're as bad as Shay. Some dogs like cats, some don't. Just like humans. And besides, I'm usually a person, not a dog."

"Do you play with her when you're all furry and four-legged?"

"Yes, Scrappy gets along very well with me when I'm Trixie."

She smiled as she gave her head a little shake. "You seriously belong here in Ugly Creek."

"Because I'm a shifter?"

"Because you're nuts." She chuckled as she snagged Scrappy and held her nose-to-nose.

I saw a glisten in Stephie's eyes, then a moment later she let go of Scrappy with one hand so she could wipe at her face.

"Are you all right?"

"I'm fine." She waved a hand in a dismissive fashion, and Scrappy reached out to bat at it. "She's just so freaking cute."

I was considering what else to say, when her cell sounded. While Stephie talked to her handsome husband, I stretched out on my stomach and focused on playing with my furball while ignoring the conversation beside me. I did hear her say something about being teary-eyed. Not my business, I told myself, and ignored the conversation.

A few minutes later, Stephie clicked off her phone. "This is fun, but I think I'd better get home."

"He misses you."

She smiled as she gave a little one-shouldered shrug. "That and he needs help with the store paperwork."

I pulled myself to my feet and walked her out to her little red car. "Thank you for the introduction."

"Good luck with your with your plan to convince Hunter to accept both sides of your personality."

"Thanks."

"Hey, isn't that the puppy that was in the woods?"

I looked where she was pointing and sure enough it was. "That's her," I said.

"She's adorable!" Stephie took a moment to wipe at her eyes and sniff, then slid into her car. "See you later."

I watched her go down the road, and once the car was around the corner I turned toward the dog. "Do you want to talk to me?"

The puppy's ears twitched. "Come over and we'll sit down and talk." She seemed to start my way, only to stop in mid-stride and head in the other direction.

A sigh on my lips, I headed back into the house.

I wandered around a few minutes, drank some water, ate a couple of cookies, and peeked out the windows about a million times. When I was fairly certain she wasn't coming back anytime soon, if at all, I stripped and shifted.

Bumpkins and I played a little while, but Miz Carlisle kept too close a watch to allow for us to really let loose. Still, it was a relief I really needed. I ran for a bit, allowing the movement to push tension and stress out of my body. I was thrilled that Shay and Ace had hit things off so well, but at times like this, I seriously missed having my cousin around to talk to.

A familiar scent caught my attention, and I turned. The teenage girl I'd seen hanging around stood at the front fence. I took my time going toward her, noticing as I did that her scent and the puppy's were similar. Sister or not, this girl was a shifter.

I sat near her on my side of the fence, hoping not to spook the skittish girl. I looked at her, she looked at me, and I figured were both wondering what next.

She looked past me and a smile lit her face. "So cute!"

By now the scent of kitten verified what I'd suspected. Scrappy had yet another admirer.

The girl sat on her heels and slowly reached her hand through the fence and toward the cat. Scrappy edged forward and rubbed her head against the girl's fingers.

"She's so soft!" The girl looked at me. "Is it okay if I pick her up?"

I nodded. She turned back to Scrappy and murmured nonsense as she took the kitty in her arms. I watched her a few minutes, enjoying the affection between my cat and a girl who just might be my sister. Sister. Boy was that a strange thought!

My possible sister glanced toward me, a big grin on her face, and warmth filled my heart. I caught her gaze and used my nose to indicate the house.

"You want to go in the house?"

I nodded.

She looked at the house for a moment, then nodded. "Can I carry kitty in?"

I nodded, gave her my best canine grin, then went to the gate and used my nose to poke at the latch. She flipped open the gate, came inside, and locked the latch back. I headed toward the house, looking back occasionally to make sure she was following, and led her to the front door. I gave a short bark and used my paw to smack the floor twice.

"You want me to wait here?"

I nodded and headed around the house to the doggie door. A couple of minutes later I had dressed and pulled open the front door.

The girl came inside and put the now squirming kitten on the floor. She took a moment to watch Scrappy run around, then stood and faced me. "So you are a shifter. Daddy said you weren't, but I didn't believe him." She held out a hand. "I'm Rose."

"Terri," I said, giving the smaller hand a squeeze. "You're a shifter too, right? I've seen a collie puppy."

She frowned. "You didn't know? I thought Daddy

would have told you."

I let out the deep sigh before it popped me like an overfilled balloon. "I've only spoken to Daddy twice since I was four, both of them within the last few days. Until then I didn't even know I had a sister."

She stood staring at me, big eyes blinking rapidly, forehead pulled into a frown. "Really? I thought it was just me he didn't like."

My heart took a dive toward my toes. Before I started asking questions, I probably should show the kid some manners. "How would you feel about a turkey sandwich?"

"I am a little hungry."

In the kitchen I loaded down the counter with sandwich makings. Rose tentatively began to put a few things on her bread.

"I don't know about you, but after I shift I'm always starving." I plopped a huge hunk of turkey on my bread and proceeded to follow that with a couple of slices of roast beef, various slices of cheese, pickle slices, a squirt of spicy mustard, and a tiny slice of tomato on top.

She grinned, and followed my lead. Our sandwiches were stacked when we sat at the kitchen table with glasses of iced tea. We both dug in with the enthusiasm only a shifter could appreciate.

"My mom says I eat like a teenage boy," she said between huge bites.

"My mom told me that too. Then she told me I would weigh a ton before I was twenty." I smiled at my sister. *My sister*. Wow that was a weird thought. "We use a huge amount of calories when we shift, so we have to eat a lot to keep going.

She glanced toward the floor and smiled, then tore a bit of meat off her sandwich and leaned down. Scrappy backed up a step once she got hold of the treat, and scarfed it down. Rose saw me watching and looked down at her plate. "I probably shouldn't have done that without asking."

"It's fine. I've spoiled her so badly she's probably beyond hope already."

Rose chuckled. "I'd love to have a cat, but we live in an apartment that doesn't allow pets."

My food caught in my throat and I took a moment to swallow it. "Wait, you live in an apartment?"

She nodded.

"Then how do you handle shifting?"

She poked a finger at her sandwich as she shrugged. "We go to a friend of Mom's, two, sometimes three, times a week. I can run in her backyard with her dogs."

I had a sudden need to have my hearing checked. Surely I didn't just hear what I think I did. "You only shift two or three times a week?"

"Sometimes not even that much, if Mom's busy or something."

Tears stung my eyes, and I blinked hard to hold them back. "That has to be really hard. If I can't shift at least a couple times a day I feel like my skin's gonna crawl off me."

Rose stared at me as her forehead pulled into a frown. "It bothers you too?"

"It's actually painful after a while."

She wiggled in her seat, looked at her hands, and bit her lower lip. "Mom says the more I shift the more I'll want to shift, until I want to stay a dog."

"Have you talked to your...to Daddy about it?"

She shook her head. "He won't talk about it."

"Is that what makes you think your...our...dad doesn't like you? Because he won't talk about shifting with you?"

"He won't talk to me about anything. He pretty much just ignores me."

"I'm sorry, Rose. He apparently has some serious father issues."

"No kidding." She locked her gaze on mine. "You said you shift a couple of times a *day*. Wow! Do you want to stay a dog all the time?"

"No. I love the feeling of being canine and running and stuff, but I like being human just as much."

Rose sighed. "It is so great to talk to somebody who knows about this shifting stuff."

"I'm not an expert or anything."

"You're a shifter. That, for sure, makes you more an expert than Mom."

Great, now I was a freaking expert. I believe a cliché involving the blind leading the blind would be appropriate here. I sighed. "I wish Daddy would talk to you. To me too, for that matter. I'm sure there are a million things he could tell us about shifting and living as a shifter and who knows what else."

I was ready to end the conversation involving our errant parental unit, and I recognized the wiggling Rose was doing. It was time to play. "Wanna go run in the backyard?"

Hope filled her eyes, making her look even younger than she was. "You mean..."

"As four-legged creatures. What do you call your canine self?"

She looked at me like I was asking what planet we were on. "What do you mean?"

My turn for confusion. "You don't call yourself by another name when you're a dog?"

"Why would I? I'm still me."

I shrugged. "In case somebody asks the dog's name. It also makes it easier to keep things straight. My canine name is Trixie."

"So I need to name the other me?"

"Only if you want to." I smiled at my beautiful sister. "Let's go running in the yard. There's a doggie door in the back door where we can come and go as we please."

I reached for the tie behind my neck to unfasten my halter top.

"You just…right here…"

A glance at her wide eyes and the bloodless color of her face had me retying my top. "I'm sorry, Rose. Shay is always telling me that not everybody is as uninhibited as I am. You can use my bedroom, it's the one on the left." I indicated the direction.

A few minutes later, Trixie greeted Rose's puppy self, and we headed out into the yard. We raced around, Rose played with Scruffy, and we even played with Bumpkins for a bit. We went easy on each other, and he was surprisingly gentle with Rose.

The sun was low on the horizon when an SUV pulled into the driveway and Ace and Shay piled out. I barked hello, and they waved toward me. I turned toward Rose, hoping I could show her off, or maybe even introduce her to our cousin and her fiancé. She had other ideas though, she'd jumped the fence and was headed toward the forest. I considered going after her. I was sure I could follow her scent. But would that just freak her out? Maybe even destroy the tiny bit of trust we'd forged? My heart twisted as I turned and walked toward the house.

Chapter Fifteen

I went in the back door and straight into my
bedroom to shift, get dressed, and put my ragged
emotions back where they belonged. When I saw
Rose's clothes folded on my bed, her sneakers sitting
neatly side by side on the floor, I realized my emotions
would be a long time in straightening out. I had a sister.
Wow!

When I joined the group again, Ace headed directly
toward me. "Do you know who that little collie belongs
to? I've seen it a couple of times, but I couldn't get a
good look, much less check for a collar."

"She's new around here." Immediately my mind
went into a tizzy wondering how much I could say
without invading Rose's privacy.

"It's her, isn't it?" Shay's eyes were huge, almost
as big as her smile. "That collie is your sister, and she's
a shifter like you."

So much for invading Rose's privacy. They were
family, though, and I knew they would accept her
without question. "Yes, that was Rose."

"We scared her off." Shay gave me a hug. "I'm
sorry."

"She's really skittish," I told her. "She took off
before I could tell her you're family."

"We'll meet her later."

"Holy double-collie, there's two of 'em."

I slugged Ace in the upper arm hard enough that he groaned. "Stuff it, human."

"Doggie breath."

I blew in his face, then turned. "I'm going outside for a bit. I'll be back."

"We'll start dinner." Shay headed for the kitchen.

Ace shifted his feet, glanced into the kitchen, then shifted some more. I chuckled. "You can relax, I'm going outside as a human."

I didn't wait for his snarky remark, I went out the back door and stood on the porch looking out toward the woods behind the house. "Rose," I said, pitching my voice so that only someone standing near me—or a canine—could hear. "I want to talk more when you feel comfortable coming back. Or I'll meet you somewhere."

When I felt the rush of tears in my eyes, I realized just how emotional I was about that adorable sister of mine. I barely knew her, and yet there was a connection between us that was incredibly strong.

A car pulled up to the front, and I could tell by the sound it was the other person I cared deeply for but wasn't sure what to do with. "At least let me know you're okay," I told the sister I loved, then turned toward the house and the man I loved.

In the kitchen, I shoved past the tangled bodies of my cousin and Ace. Starting dinner, my left paw. I rolled my eyes, but there was a smile on my face. I loved my cousin, and if Ace made her happy, then that was fine with me.

I pulled open the door just as Hunter started a second round of knocking. "Sorry," I told him. "I had to shove past the Shay and Ace meld in the kitchen."

Hunter grabbed me and plastered my body against his. "Like this?" He whispered against my lips, then proceeded to kiss me until I was floating a mile in the air on a cloud of happiness.

"Aren't they cute?" Shay said.

"Charming," Ace said.

We looked toward the couple standing in the kitchen door. "We are, aren't we?" Hunter grinned.

"Aren't you supposed to be making dinner?" I asked.

They looked deeply into each other's eyes. "We were thinking about maybe just getting tacos."

I narrowed my eyes at them. "You two have to go get them."

"We will," Ace said. "In a minute." He pulled Shay against him, locked his lips against hers, and I buried my face in Hunter's chest. Laughter rumbled through him.

"We're going to starve," Hunter said.

I looked up at him. "Doesn't that new Chinese place deliver?"

He raised an eyebrow. "They do."

I looked behind me to find Ace in the overstuffed chair and Shay in his lap. I raised my gaze to the ceiling and asked, "Anything special from the Chinese place?"

There was a muttered, "Whatever," and an "Anything," from the chair's direction.

Hunter and I went out on the porch so the people who took our order wouldn't think we were watching a porn film. Okay, okay, it wasn't that bad, but it was getting to be a little much.

On the other hand, for once, Miz Carlisle watching us didn't bother me. I had way too much on my mind to care what an old biddy thought. Like my odd and confusing family, for instance.

Hunter and I sat side by side in the white wooden chairs and held hands. He smiled at me with a warmth and caring that I wouldn't have imagined I could get from anybody. Now I was sitting beside this handsome, intelligent man who I loved with all my heart. If only I knew he could accept who I really am.

A car pulled up, and Hunter squeezed my hand gently before he got up to pay the delivery guy. He carried the food, and I opened the front door about an inch.

"Food's here," I yelled. We waited until the giggling and fabric rustling stopped, then I yelled, "Coming in!"

I waited a slow count of ten, then stepped into the room. The couple was still in the chair, smiling at us, and trying hard to look innocent. Ace's hair stood straight up, Shay's top was on backward, and they both looked like they'd just had the best dessert of their lives. Innocent? Not so much.

We all sat on the floor around the coffee table. The food was good, especially considering it was Chinese and we were basically in the middle of nowhere. The world is a small place these days.

Conversation was easy and fun, and I especially enjoyed Ace teasing Hunter about his propensity for sci-fi costumes. When he pulled out a classic red fez, I had to bite my lip to keep from laughing.

"Give me my fez back." Hunter stuck the thing on his head.

I laughed in spite of myself. He didn't appear to be insulted though, he just went back to eating as if nothing had changed. Thankfully, I managed to keep my reaction down to a giggle.

Hunter raised his eyebrow at me, shrugged, and launched into a story about Ace going behind a bush for privacy, only to come running toward the rest of the group, holding his pants to keep from tripping on them, and screaming like a little girl.

"You'd scream too if you'd damn near sat on a rattlesnake."

Shay's eyes widened into softballs. "There are rattlesnakes in South America?"

"The most dangerous kind," Hunter said. "They have two types of venom, whereas most rattlesnakes only carry one."

A shiver ran down my back. "I'm glad you're okay, Ace."

"It was rather unnerving."

"Thank God you both got out safe," Shay said.

"I second that." I put my hand on Hunter's arm and squeezed.

"I'm fine," he said. "Especially now that I have my fez back."

Shay got to her feet, went to the stereo, and music began to play. I recognized the radio station; they played an eclectic mix of songs ranging from Fifties' tear-jerkers to current hits.

"Let's dance," she said, and began pulling the coffee table to the side to make more space. The rest of us had little choice but to assist her.

The space clearing quickly become a more ambitious furniture moving. Being that there was only so much room for the four of us, I decided to switch gears and finished cleaning up the dinner mess. I grabbed the garbage, danced and dodged around the other three, and headed into the kitchen.

My feet were moving to the rhythm as I dumped the garbage outside in the big container and headed back into the house. I was still tapping my toes as I washed my hands, picked up a big plate of cookies, and turned toward the party.

The first notes of a classic rock and roll song sounded as I stepped back into the living room, and the sight that greeted me almost caused me to drop dessert.

Hunter was on his feet, not just dancing, but seriously getting into the experience. His neck moved back and forth as his chin went out and back, like a chicken. His long limbs waved like crazy, and on another man would look silly. Hunter Devereux looked anything but silly. The man was graceful in a relaxed, and extremely masculine way. Holy sexy dancer man!

He saw me, danced over, took the plate from me and put it on the coffee table. He grabbed my hand and pulled me into the cleared floor space. It was freaky at first. I'd never danced with anyone so uninhibited, but as soon as I got past that first odd jolt, I had an amazing time. After all, Shay keeps saying I'm the most uninhibited person she knows. It stood to reason that Hunter and I could put everybody else to shame with our crazy moves.

The music stopped, and I would have been disappointed if I could breathe.

"Did I embarrass you?" Hunter asked.

"Hell no," I told him. We smiled a secret message to each other, conveying the fun we'd had and the affection we felt for each other.

A slow song was playing, and I realized Shay and

Ace were wrapped around each other as they rocked back and forth together. Hunter's strong arms tugged me against a warm, firm body, and I let myself go as we moved slowly to the rhythm.

Hunter held me close, one hand slowly sliding down to cup my rear. I gasped and he chuckled. The sound of a moan had me looking around to see who'd seen what, only to realize sweet and handsome had his back turned to the other couple, so nobody saw anything. My heart warmed, inciting my body to lean against him a little more firmly. I groaned.

"We have to go do that thing," Shay's voice said. I peeked around Hunter and realized Ace had a hand inside her top.

"Yeah, um, I have to meet a guy," Ace said, his voice tight.

Shay grabbed her purse, and they stumbled out the door.

They were gone, probably to Ace's house. I tried to keep a handle on my feelings, but excitement swirled through me anyway. We were alone, just Hunter and me.

Scrappy mewed to remind me of her presence. I smiled and gave her a quick tummy rub. "I know you're there, kitty."

Hunter locked the front door, and I glanced out the front window at the crazy neighbor in her flower garden. She watched our house intently, as she'd done every damn day since Shay and I moved in.

Hunter came up behind me and slipped his arms around my waist. "Still sore?" He whispered.

"Not really."

"I don't want to hurt you."

"I want you." Damn, my voice was shaking.

I turned and he put his hand against my cheek. "I'll be careful, sweetheart."

"I trust you."

He closed his eyes for a moment, and a smile pulled at his mouth when he once again met my gaze. "That's the nicest thing anybody ever said to me."

He picked me up and took me into my bedroom where he put me on the bed and slid in on top of me. "My precious Terri," he said as he slipped my top over my head.

I wondered if he'd feel the same way after I forced the truth on him.

Chapter Sixteen

Hunter and I walked through the forest, hand—in-hand, the sound of birds and small animals all around us. The breeze was fresh, if rather chilly to my Florida-raised blood. Hunter's hand was warm, and that's all I needed to be comfortable enough.

"This is nice," Hunter said. "I think you made up that story about wanting to show me something just so you could get me alone in the woods."

"Rats, you're on to me."

He stopped and put his hands on my upper arms so he could pull me close. "You brought me out here to ravish me, didn't you?"

My heart beat hard in my chest. My body and his seemed to be calling for each other, something inside both of us longing not just for physical connection, but something far deeper, something that had the potential to tie us together on a different plane.

His lips covered mine, and the stuffing vanished from my legs. He pulled me close, wrapped his arms around me, and held me upright so that he could kiss me more thoroughly.

"Hunter," I gasped. His hands roamed down over my lower back and onto the swell of my rear. I tried to focus on the mission, but my thoughts were scrambled. I managed a pathetic shove to his chest, but he didn't believe I wanted him to stop. Mostly because I didn't.

Then out of the corner of my eye, I saw Abukcheech waiting near a big tree. I had to stop groping at Hunter like a teenager and use this opportunity. This had to work, there were too many things hanging in the balance for it to fail.

With a big sigh, I shoved Hunter back an inch. "Stop. Please. I really do have something to show you."

He stopped his efforts to scramble my brain cells. "What is it you want to show me in the middle of the woods?"

I swallowed hard. "Something I hope will convince you of the reality of things you can't explain."

He gave a little snort. "There are a lot of things I can't explain."

"Things science can't explain."

"You're welcome to try."

I motioned for my friend, and he headed for us. Hunter turned to see, and I heard his sharp intake of breath.

"This is Abukcheech," I told him. "He's a real, live Bigfoot."

Hunter spun to face me so fast and hard I took a step backward. "What the hell do you think you're doing?"

I did my best to ignore what looked to be anger in his face, and somehow managed a tiny smile. "Proving that Bigfoot exists."

"Do you think I'm stupid?"

What the hell? "No, of course not. What are you talking about?"

"Did you really think you could trick me with a guy in a Halloween costume?" He waved a hand in the direction of Abukcheech, then turned and stomped back the way we'd come.

I was left standing there with my mouth hanging open.

"Man not happy? Abukcheech asked.

"Man needs kick in the rear."

I heard a deep chuckle and turned to look at my furry friend.

"Humans very odd." The Bigfoot youngster turned and headed deeper into the woods.

I took the long way home. I had a lot to think about, and some hard crying to do.

****

I didn't hear anything from Hunter that night. I did spend a lot of time on one porch or the other, calling softly for Rose. Asking her to please let me know she was all right. About midnight, I shifted and headed out to track down my sister's scent. She had been all over the neighborhood, not that I hadn't pretty much figured that out anyway. I circled until I found a trace leading away from Aunt Ruth's house and toward the foot of the mountain.

There were a lot of various animal smells here, some domestic, most not. Rose's scent meandered around, going near small shacks that were being used mostly for storage and one apparently the home of an old man who sat on the porch in an old wooden chair. A shotgun lay on the porch near him. He was the cliché of hillbilly hermit, which would be interesting if Rose wasn't out here somewhere. My head hurt at the thought of my little sister alone so far from her home.

Shock tore through my nerves as I realized I didn't even know where Rose lived when she wasn't wandering the countryside looking for the sister who didn't even know about her. How crazy was my life? I had to find her, I had to know she was all right. I might not have known about her until a few days ago, but she was family. And I was going to make sure we stayed in touch from now on.

I followed my nose down a rutted dirt road toward the sound of a stream. The smell of wood burning had me thinking there was a house of some kind back in the area partially hidden by a hill. Was she staying there? Alone? I shivered at the thought.

I smelled him just before the big black dog came rushing from the thick foliage near the stream. My instinct was to run, but thoughts of my baby sister had me holding my ground. I moved into a fighting stance, letting a deep growl grow in the back of my throat. I wanted to ask this guy about Rose, but when a male dog's in perimeter guarding mode there isn't really a way to get him to listen. Something that, in my opinion, they share with human males.

He edged my way, his rear low to the ground, his ears back, his growl harsh and unfriendly. He did not want me there, and I'd never developed my defensive skills. I'm a collie after all. We're herders, not fighters.

It slowly sunk into my thick head that I might have to get away while I could and come back later, preferably with help. Only the thought of Rose had me holding my ground and wondering if there was some way to make this guy understand

A high-pitched bark startled me, and I shot my gaze away from the black dog for a microsecond, just long enough to see Rose coming up from behind the black dog. I tried to warn her away, but she headed toward him like an arrow. I was shaking hard, but I managed to run toward them, letting out a warning growl as I went.

I was preparing to jump between Rose and the black dog, when I realized she was talking to him. Not talking in the way of humans, but with a combination of scent, body language, and a bit of psychic ability. Yeah, dogs are psychic. I'll put that on my list of things to freak out Hunter with. Provided he ever speaks to me again.

Now that I realized they knew each other, I slowed my approach. I wanted to give the black dog time to recognize me as a friend. Or at least that's how I hoped he'd think of me.

Rose turned to look at me, barked, turned back to him, and barked again. He lowered his head, gave me a glance that wasn't entirely friendly, and sent me a message that I'd better not hurt Rose. I immediately liked him.

Rose was giving me a hard glare, so I indicated we go somewhere and talk. She thought about it for a moment, then turned back to black dog. He gave me another 'don't hurt Rose look, then turned and walked away.

Rose and I walked for a minute or so before she ducked into the bushes and shifted. "What do you want?" she asked from behind foliage that concealed her nudity.

I moved into the bushes myself before I shifted, then made sure my personal parts stayed covered. "To make sure you're okay," I told her. "I'd like you to come back to Aunt Ruth's house with me."

"So you can call Daddy to come and get me?"

Wow, this girl had some serious anger issues. Not

that I blamed her.

"No. I wouldn't do that.

"Why should I believe you?"

I put my hands on my hips and let my own anger come to the surface. "Because I hadn't seen Daddy since I was four years old. Well, three actually, he left before my birthday. Because he never bothered to tell me I have a sister, and I want a chance to get to know her." I swiped my eyes before I met her gaze again. "Come with me. Let's get to know each other. Together we'll figure out what to do."

"Who were those people who came to your house?"

"Shay is our cousin. She's staying at Aunt Ruth's house with me. And Ace is her fiancé. I wanted to introduce you, but you took off.

She studied me for a moment, as if trying to decide if I was on the level. Finally she nodded. "Okay, I'll go with you. Just let me go say bye to Charger."

Five minutes later, we were headed home. Just knowing that Rose was safe was enough to cause me to be shaky. How I'd become so attached to the girl in such a short time was beyond me.

Then she sent a doggie smile my way, and I realized that we might not have known of each other's existence, but we were sisters, and that fact connected us in a strong, special way.

Back at the house, we went in the doggie door and I shifted right there in the kitchen. I grabbed for the bathrobe and slipped it on so as not to embarrass her. "Your clothes are still in the bedroom, if you want to shift." I shrugged. "If not, no problem."

She went down the hall, and I put together a snack.

When she came back, as Rose the human and dressed in her cute blue shorts and matching blue and white top, I handed her a plate and indicated the fixings I'd put on the table. "Hope you like nachos."

"I love nachos." She wasted no time putting together a plate of food. Then, like me, she sat at the table and dug in."

"So you've been hanging out with that dog?"

"Charger? Yeah, he's an old dude, but sweet."

"You've been getting enough to eat?"

She looked at the chip as she poked it at her cheese. "There's a woman, Granny May, who lives in a little house back in the woods. People, mostly women, come to see her for herbs and stuff. They talk about her when she isn't around, saying she's a witch and stuff. I think she's an exceptional herbalist and they just don't recognize her talent."

My curiosity rose to the surface. "How do you know about herbalists?"

"Mom. She's always reading about different healing stuff. She tried a lot of different herbs and compounds from the time Daddy said I might be able to shift—if I got the gene—until a few months ago. I had a bad time with a nasty brown mix, threw up for three days. She finally had to take me to the doctor and act all innocent like she had no idea why I was so sick." The chip in Rose's hand crumpled into little pieces.

"Why in the world would she give you—" Before the words were out I knew why. "To stop you from shifting."

"She says it's an illness like muscular dystrophy or cystic fibrosis or something. She believes there is a cure out there somewhere, and she is dead set on finding it."

My heart shattered into a million pieces. "Oh, my sweet Rose! No, being a shifter is just part of who you are. I love being able to run through the grass, to chase butterflies, to see the world from a completely different perspective."

She was smiling. "I think so too. And so did the Granny May in the woods."

Well that stopped my thought train. "You told her about your ability?"

"No, she figured it out. I have no idea how. And no, she didn't see me shift."

Like Ms. Funderburk had with me. "Our scent, I think, is what gives us away."

"We smell funny?" Rose's scrunched up nose had me smiling.

"No, but we do have a different scent than non-shifters. That's what Shay and I figured out was the most likely giveaway. And Abukcheech said I smelled like dog, but humans apparently can't smell that."

Her face lit up. "Abukcheech is that Bigfoot you met?"

"Yep."

"Could you introduce me?"

"Of course." I touched her arm. "So, this herbalist was impressed with your ability?"

Rose smiled. "I guess. She told me I was special and that I should be proud of what I am."

"She's not wrong. You're a special girl, Rose." I grinned. "Plus you have this cool ability to shift into a cute puppy."

"I'm not a puppy. I'm a grown-up dog."

"Oh, you're still a puppy. You're only fourteen."

Her lower lip slid into a pout. "Mom won't be

happy about that. She says my dog is too big now."

"You're a collie. We aren't little dogs. Woof!"

She giggled. "I'm so glad I came here."

"I'd have come to you if I'd known about you."

She abruptly threw her arms around me. Tears stung my eyes as I hugged her close. When she let go, I saw the dark circles under her eyes. Some protective big sister I was. "Let's get some rest."

"Okay."

"I can sleep on the couch and you can have my bed."

She nodded, but without raising her gaze. I tipped her chin up. "What's wrong, sweetie?"

"It's silly. Mom thinks I'm weird, but I guess I hoped maybe, because you're a shifter too…"

"Out with it, little sis. I seriously doubt you're anywhere near as weird as I am."

Her smile was weak, but she spoke. "I like to, you know, snuggle. Mom says people are going to think I'm…strange."

My lips pulled into a smile. "People, maybe. We're partly dogs, and dogs sleep in piles of snuggles."

"You too?"

I nodded. "And you just corroborated I'm normal—for a half-woman half-collie, anyway. Thanks!"

I found her a big T-shirt to sleep in, and we snuggled into my bed. One part of my life was good. Now if I could just figure out how to deal with Hunter.

****

The next morning we went back to where Rose had been staying to collect her backpack from where she'd stashed it and to tell Charger and Granny May she was going with me. Then we went into town to buy her some extra clothes and supplies.

"You have to meet Stephie," I told her. "She's interesting."

She narrowed her eyes, but still went with me into the antique store.

Stephie saw us as soon as we walked in, and came our way. "Hi, I'm Stephie." She held out a hand to Rose. "You have got to be related to Terri. You two look an awful lot alike."

"This is my sister Rose. Rose, this is my good friend Stephie."

"It's nice to meet you."

The bell over the door sounded, and Stephie's eyes widened. I knew who was behind me without turning. I'd know that spicy, male scent anywhere.

"Rose, I have some things I'd like to show you. Let's give your sister some space, okay?"

Rose looked more like she wanted to grab me and run, but she went with Stephie.

I turned. "Hello, Hunter."

"Terri." He took a step toward me. "I think I might have been a little harsh yesterday."

I forced my left shoulder into a little shrug. "Whatever."

He moved closer. "Look, there's no way what you showed me could be anything other than a man in a costume. It isn't logical."

"So you're saying *if* you don't believe in something *then* that something can't possibly exist?"

"No." He rubbed his fingers over his forehead. "Just that some things are impossible."

I took a step toward him this time. "You said

yourself that Bigfoot might be some sort of previously unknown animal, and therefore their existence might be possible."

"Why is this crazy stuff so important to you? Most people never even seriously consider the possibility of the existence of ghosts or faeries, or Bigfoot. Why are you obsessed with the idea?"

"More like you're obsessed with not believing."

His eyes flashed, and his jaw tightened. "Why can't we just have a normal relationship like everybody else?"

I leaned close to him. "Because we aren't everybody else." I spun so my back was to him and marched off.

When I passed Rose and Stephie, I gave them a quick wave. "I need a minute." And I headed off to the little bathroom in the back of the store.

When I came back out Hunter was gone and Rose was waiting to hug me. "Are you all right?"

"More or less."

"I take it your plan didn't work," Stephie said.

"Nope."

"I'm sorry."

"What plan?" Rose asked.

I sighed "The one to force him to believe in something you can't prove in a laboratory."

Rose's eyes filled with tears. "He doesn't understand you."

"He doesn't know me." I dropped onto one of the stools at the counter. "I'm afraid to tell him I'm a shapeshifter."

"Why?" Rose asked.

I looked into her innocent little face and smiled.

"Because I'm afraid he'd freak. Or maybe just not believe his eyes. He seems to be very good at that denial thing."

"Believing he saw a Bigfoot is one thing. I think it would be really hard to deny seeing a person shift into a dog." She glanced toward Stephie. "You didn't have any trouble believing, did you?"

Stephie's lips pulled into a smile. "You were the puppy in the woods. I knew there was something familiar about you. And no, seeing is definitely believing."

I was considering that, when the shop door opened and Ace rushed in with Shay right behind him. "We saw your car and thought you might be here." He was breathing hard, as if he'd run.

"What's wrong?"

"You're my cousin," Shay grinned at Rose.

"Not exactly," Rose said.

"Close enough!" Shay pulled Rose into her arms.

Ace had my arm and pulled me to one side. "I just saw Hunter."

I nodded. "He came in here. He's not happy that I don't get my facts from a microscope slide like he does."

"He's leaving, Terri."

A huge bolder dropped hard on the bottom of my stomach. "Leaving? What do you mean?"

"He told me his agent called him and that guy who hacked into six banks wants a ghostwriter—but Hunter would have to go to California now. Today"

"As in not even telling me?" Then I realized he probably was trying, in his own way.

"He said he's crazy about you, but he doesn't think

the two of you have a chance." Ace touched my arm. "He said it might be easier if he just left. I tried to tell him he's an idiot, but he isn't good at listening."

The urge to beat Hunter into pulp was so strong I headed for the door.

Ace moved to block my way. "He's gone to the B&B to pack."

It took a moment for my brain to register what my friend was telling me, but when it did I wasted no time grabbing Ace's arm and pulling him over to the others. "Shay, will you and Ace take care of Rose for a bit? I have something I need to do."

Rose crossed her arms over her chest and narrowed her eyes. "I don't need a babysitter."

"Of course not," Shay said. "You need to be with family so we can get to know each other."

I put a hand on either side of Rose's face. "Please stay with them. I need to know you'll be safe. I'll be back as soon as I can."

"Go," she said. "You love him. You can't just let him go without a fight."

"Thanks." I looked back toward the other three. "I'll let you know something as soon as I can."

I hugged everybody, Rose twice, and headed toward the door.

Chapter Seventeen

I didn't really expect Hunter to answer, but he could at least let me know he'd received one of the texts or voice mails I'd sent him over the last two hours. I was standing in my living room at the moment, wishing for my phone to ring. My nerves danced on each other and I would go to him if I had to, but I really preferred to do this in private.

Fear that he would just go without talking to me finally convinced me to go to the B&B. I locked the doggie door to keep Scrappy inside while I was gone, and was ready to charge off on my mission when a knock all but scared the shoes off me. I swallowed hard, sent up a prayer, and pulled open the door. It was Hunter, and he did not look happy.

"Okay, I'm here. What's so important that I need to know?"

"Come on in."

He sighed and leaned against the door frame for a moment before he came into the living room.

"Have a seat."

"No."

Shock had me frozen in mid-movement. "Your choice," I finally managed. "There's something about me that you don't know. Something I was afraid to tell you."

"Are you sick?"

The concern in his expression assured me he still cared, but would caring be enough?

"No, I'm healthy. But there is something about me that I didn't think you'd believe. I should have just told you, but I was hoping I could convince you to be a little more open-minded before I did."

He sighed hard and long. "Let me guess, you're psychic."

I rolled my eyes. "If I was psychic, I would know how you're going to react and I wouldn't be so worried."

"Just tell me what it is, okay? I have to be on a plane California in less than six hours."

I wanted to scream. How could he just brush what we had off like that? Tears threatened, but I refused to allow them to leave my eyes. "I have to show you."

"Okay."

"I'm going to prove you're wrong not to believe in things beyond what is considered rational."

Hunter rolled his eyes. "We've already been through this."

"There's no way you can call this fake."

Arms crossed over his chest, he stood waiting. "Bring it on."

I backed up a step and pulled my T-shirt over my head. My jeans hit the floor and I reached around to unfasten my bra.

"I don't know what you're doing," Hunter said. "But so far I like it."

It hit me right in the belly. This was the point of no return. I could stop now, tell him I was teasing, let him finish undressing me, then apologize in bed. That was the kind of thing full-humans did. I doubted he'd question my motives. If I kept going, there would be no going back. I could lose him forever.

"Let me guess, your undies are going to disappear."

I looked into his amazing eyes, and knew that if he wasn't willing to take me the way I was, there was no hope for us anyway. My bra hit the floor, followed by my panties. I could smell the desire coming off him, and wished fervently that was the goal. "I love you," I said, watching as his eyes widened and his forehead pulled into a frown.

I reached into myself and let my body shift. Seconds later, I looked up at him from the eyes of a collie.

Hunter's breath sucked in, and a sudden blast of the scent of fear hit me. He backed away. "What are you?" he gasped. He backed up and almost fell over the coffee table. Using his hands to feel his way, and without taking his gaze off me, he moved to the door, opened it, and ran across the porch.

I shifted back to human as fast as I could and rushed outside. He was already closing the door of his car. He met my gaze and the horror in his eyes tore at my heart. He backed out of the driveway, and I knew I had just lost the one man I would ever give my heart to, one of the handful of people who knew what I really was.

Which apparently was a monster, if his reaction was anything to go by.

I heard a noise, and saw Miz Carlisle, her eyes narrowed, glaring hard at me. "I'm calling the police," she said.

She had no idea how little I cared at the moment.

"Have at it," I told her. She gasped as I went into the house.

There I stood, in a house belonging to my aunt. I had no place of my own, two close friends, including Shay—and she was family. A little sister I couldn't even take care of. I wouldn't even be able to take care of myself without the career I apparently had lost the talent for. I knew that wasn't exactly true, but it felt true.

I went into my bedroom, or rather the bedroom my aunt had invited me to use, and pulled on jeans and a T-shirt. I sat on the side of the bed and tried to think. Mom and Shay both said I tended to be irresponsible, so I guessed I owed it to myself to consider everything as carefully as I could.

A few minutes later, I pulled out my suitcase and stated throwing in clothes. By the time the sun was sliding behind those gorgeous Tennessee hills, I was ready to go. I took a look around. I had my clothes and personal items in my suitcase. I also had a bag with water bottles and snacks. My debit and credit cards were in my wallet, I had my keys. Phone and charger. I'd get a few dollars from the ATM on my way.

My gaze went to the laptop sitting on my desk. I should take that.

No. There was no reason. That part of my life was over, and the best thing I could do was let it go. Somewhere deep inside, my logic circuit argued that wasn't true, that I was making a catastrophe out of a setback. I ignored that idea, because I couldn't imagine ever writing again, it had been hard enough before. Now, without Hunter in my life, it seemed like counting the stars in the sky would be easier. So I left the laptop.

I grabbed my e-reader, and a few magazines I hadn't taken the time to read. I stuffed those into a tote bag I'd gotten at a conference, picked everything up, told Scruffy I'd call Shay to take care of her, and headed for the door.

I locked my aunt's house, got into my car and sat for a time looking at my old life. I had to have some time and space alone so I could figure out where I was going from there. I couldn't think while I was knee-deep in the mess I'd made of my life.

I backed out and drove away from Ugly Creek toward the Interstate. I didn't know what lay ahead of me, and I was seriously reluctant to find out. I stopped to get gas and took time to call Shay. "Would you mind feeding Scrappy and keeping an eye on Rose for a couple of days?"

"Of course I don't mind. I take it things didn't work out."

"No."

"I'm sorry, sweetie."

"Just take care of my sister, okay. Don't let her run away, and don't let Daddy know where she is. Something is not right, and I want to know what it is before I let her go home."

"You know you don't have any legal rights to protect her."

"I'll worry about that when I find out what's actually going on. Just keep her safe and tell her I love her, okay?"

"Okay. You be careful."

"I will."

I hung up and headed northeast.

Chapter Eighteen

I love the Smoky Mountains where the air is fresh and the views are breathtaking. In the summer, every little town is filled with vacationers. In the winter, snow skiers head to the few resorts. Right now, the place was packed with seekers of autumn color. Unfortunately, when I had the bright idea to come up here, I didn't factor in the autumn-in-the-mountains deluge. Comes from living in Florida my whole life, I guess.

Instead of following the crowd to Gatlinburg, I kept driving across I-40 to Asheville, North Carolina. I'd never been there, but I'd seen pictures of the town years ago, and ever since then I'd wanted to visit.

The city, and the big mountains surrounding it, were more beautiful than I'd expected them to be. The sun was getting low in the sky, shooting light between trees and buildings. The bright colors of autumn leaves glowed and I caught myself wishing Hunter was with me to enjoy the show together.

I ignored the pain thinking about him provoked and drove around until I found a three-star chain hotel fairly close to the forest. I checked in, paced around in the room for a while, then gave in to my nature. There was forest everywhere, making my life easy. I drove to a parking area near a promising site and hiked a little way, scoping out the territory. Then I stashed clothes and the car and room keys in a small bag, hid the bag under a rock, and let my body do its thing. Running through the thick expanse of trees was amazing. Fresh air blew gently over my fur while sun and shade created a living checkerboard. The scents were incredible. The warm, grounding smell of earth, the sweet aroma of late blooming flowers, the tangy smell of leaves as their colors shifted and they fell gracefully to the ground.

I gave chase to a tiny frog, but the game didn't last long. I didn't want to scare the poor thing. A squirrel offered a much more interesting hunt. There was no question of scaring that guy as we twisted and turned around trees, bushes, stumps, rocks. Sometimes I rushed after him, sometimes he went after me. Finally he climbed halfway up a tall oak and turned upside down to tell me he had a wife and baby to get home to. We thanked each other, and I headed out for more adventure before I turned back toward my human life.

I barely slept that night. I missed Rose. I missed Hunter. I missed Shay. I even missed Ace and his teasing. I missed getting up before daylight to play make-believe with my computer. Writing fiction was a lot of fun, and the knowledge that my readers were able to share in my made-up world was amazing. I wanted that ability back.

****

To top off my sleepless night, just before five a.m. my phone buzzed its way across the nightstand. I grabbed at it, fear wrenching my heart as I did. Was something wrong with Rose? Had Daddy grabbed her? Or was it Shay? Had something happened to her?

I blinked the blur from my eyes, and it was Hunter's name that lit up the display. Well, he was the very last person I wanted to talk to, so I sent him to voice mail, returned my phone to the nightstand, and closed my eyes. There was no real reason for me to get out of bed, so I'd just stay where I was.

I was dozing a bit when the thing vibrated again. I checked just to be sure, then sent him to voice mail again. "Leave me alone, Devereux."

I knew he wouldn't though. There was no way I was going to get any sleep, so I slid out of bed to get ready for whatever this day would bring. Not that I had a lot of interest in the possibilities, but my other choice would be to lie in bed and feel sorry for myself. That was not going to happen. My life as a writer might be over, but my body was used to getting up before daylight.

While I dressed and put on a bit of makeup, the phone did one vibrating dance after another over the surface of the table. By the time I was finished, there were fifteen voice messages, every single one of them from Hunter.

I was freaked out and a little worried about his trying so hard to get in touch with me. On the other hand, if something was truly wrong he could get in touch with Ace, and he or Shay could call me.

The probability was he was calling to beg me to explain how I did my "trick." That realization blew hot coals through my body. I'd check in with Shay later to be sure, but I wasn't going to let him know that I cared.

Right now I was starving. I stuck my annoying phone in my purse, grabbed it and my keys, and headed out to find breakfast.

I ate, drove around some, poked around a couple of stores, then eventually found my way back to my hotel.

I was always complaining that I didn't have time to read. Well, now I did. Sprawled across the big bed, I dove headfirst into the newest novel by my favorite writer.

Three hours later, I was thirsty enough to go looking for a drink machine. Hunter still haunted my thoughts, but the author had somehow managed to suck me into her fictional world and hold me there. Amazing.

My cola, my e-reader, and I settled into a chair on the large wooden balcony outside my room. The air was fresh, the breeze chilly, the leaves the warm shades of autumn, the mountains rose magnificently just a mile or so from the hotel. I'd go back there later. I'd shift and play and let the animal inside me shove aside the human worry and pain for a time. Or at least that was the plan.

With a sigh, I picked up my e-reader and slipped back into a time and place pulled not from reality, but from the mind of a writer just like me.

Well, not like me. This author's ebooks were selling at an incredible pace. As I lost myself in her world, I contemplated why my work wasn't nearly as good. Hunter had taken the time to read my stuff; he'd told me the hard facts, as he saw them, and I should at least consider what he'd said.

I couldn't though, I couldn't trust him. His mind was too unyielding. He literally couldn't see beyond what he believed. Maybe someone could help me figure out what went wrong with my work, but it was highly unlikely that person would be Dr. Hunter Devereux, professor of literature—and killer of young writers' dreams.

With that, I swung my feet to the ground and went back into my room. It would be dark soon, and I could more easily go into the woods and run like the wild animal that lived in my DNA. All our DNAs actually, but it lived closer to the surface in shifters like me. Like Rose. I missed my sister, but I had to think things through. I had to decide what the best path for me was before I could be the kind of sister she needed me to be.

I grabbed my little "go shift" bag, locked up my room, and headed for my car. Maybe my canine mind would clear my human one enough I could see the problem more clearly. At the very least, maybe I could wear myself out enough to sleep.

Chapter Nineteen

I ran through the dark forest. With not even quite a half moon, it would be all but impossible for a human to see much of anything. Luckily, my dog half didn't have that problem. I ran for hours, enjoying the fresh air, the plants I'd rarely—or never—seen before, communing with the wild animals who lived there. I thoroughly enjoyed being out there, and I decided a long vacation here would be a great way to relax.

Just a vacation, though. It didn't really appeal to me, this life. Not long-term. I missed the conveniences of the twenty-first century. But most of all I missed my family. And Hunter.

Damn that man!

I sat on the soft ground and scratched my ear. I didn't trust Hunter's professor mind to be right about my work, but something about what he'd said had bothered me, made my muse twitch. Why couldn't I remember what it was? Oh yeah, it was that same handsome professor and his stubborn inability to see what was right in front of him.

I ran around for a few more minutes, then headed back to where I'd hidden my clothes. After a fast food run for enough to feed a small army, or one hungry shapeshifter, I headed back to my hotel room.

When I pulled my phone out of my bag, I realized the battery was dead. Annoyed at myself for not charging the thing, I dug out the charger and plugged it in. I shoved in some much needed food while I gave the cell a moment to start charging. When I turned it on, I saw three calls from Shay. With a groan, I called her.

"So you haven't flown off to Planet Dog after all," Shay's voice came through the phone.

"Everything okay back in Ugly Creek?"

"We're all fine, including that cute new cousin of mine."

I smiled. "She is pretty awesome, isn't she? Thanks for taking care of her."

"She's having a great time. She plays with the dogs at Ace's, then we go to Aunt Ruth's and she plays with Scrappy. She plays with the demon cat too. I was worried about her at first, but she can hold her own."

I smiled. "That's my girl."

"I don't know what we'll do if your dad shows up, though."

"If he does, just try to stall him. I'll be home soon, I promise." One way or the other.

"The only problem around here is that boyfriend of yours."

What the hell? "Hunter? He's not my boyfriend."

"Whatever he is, he's having a fit. He calls, he comes by, he's obviously very upset."

My heart did a shameful little dance. "I thought he'd gone to California?"

"Nope, he stayed here." Shay sighed. "I can't figure out if he's scared you've been possessed by a dog, eaten by a dog, you possessed a dog, you ate a dog, or if he needs you with him when he checks himself into the mental hospital."

"Oh good grief."

"What I do know is that he's afraid he's lost you for good."

"Why? Because he can't explain how I became Trixie? Tell him a magician doesn't reveal how she does her tricks."

"Being a little hard on him, aren't you? You said yourself, it's scary to see somebody you care for shift."

"Yeah, well it's hard to watch the man you love run screaming from you."

"Ouch."

"Yep."

"Look, I know this is hard for you, Terri, but the man is obviously miserable. I doubt he's eaten or slept since you revealed your furrier side."

I tried to swallow the lump forming in my throat. "He's really that upset?"

"Yes, he is. No matter what you decide to do, you know I'll support you. As your cousin and friend, I advise you to think about the situation very carefully. Remember, you told me to give Ace time, and you were right."

We hung up, and I reheated my food in the room's microwave. Nothing tasted very good, but I was hungry enough to eat anyway. Was I being too hard on Hunter? I had forced the truth down his throat. There was a part of me that argued his inability to believe had something to do with his father, and that his reaction to my shift might have come gift wrapped with his dad's disapproval.

I flipped off the light and fell onto the bed. My head was pounding and my broken heart was trying hard to grow some hope. "Don't," I told the organ. "You'll just get torn apart again."

I closed my eyes. I'd lie there until I felt better, then I'd head back home. There was no sense in hiding out. I had to go home and face the disaster my life had turned into.

****

Over the next few hours, I slept better than I had in a while. Hunter was somehow nearby, and I felt his support. Meanwhile dreams swirled and danced in my mind. Twisting and slipping from one bit to another, the images played a song for me, leaving a blueprint in my mind when I woke to darkness. As I pulled myself from sleep, a book I wanted badly to write came together—puzzle pieces sliding into place. It was different from anything I'd ever seriously considered writing. It would take a lot of work, but I knew what was wrong with the women's fiction series. I didn't have many women friends. I was making up stories from bits and pieces, and my material was getting scarce. I wanted to write scary. It was much easier to make that up. In fact, ideas were swirling around in my head like flies in the summer.

I couldn't wait to get started, but my laptop was miles away, and I didn't want to take the chance of losing the vision. I had to start as soon as I could. I'd have to do this the old-fashioned way.

I swirled and spat out mouthwash, ran a brush through my hair, and pulled on my sneakers. It was cold outside, and I was shivering by the time I got to my Fiat. It wasn't until I got in the car and saw two on my dashboard clock that I realized it was seriously early morning. What would be open? Gas stations, yes, but I really wanted a better choice than that. Then I saw the sign: Walmart. Open twenty-four hours, and had everything a writer could need.

I bought two packs of my favorite ballpoints, assorted notebooks, sticky-notes, snacks, a bright purple pair of ear buds for my MP3 player, and a pack of colorful paper clips just because I liked them. As I headed toward the checkout, I saw a nice shawl and grabbed it too. This Florida girl was cold.

Back at my hotel room, I made a cup of tea and made use of my pretty new supplies.

****

I looked up blearily to see bright sunshine cutting sideways through the window and across my hotel room. The annoying buzzing sounded again, and I stumbled to where I'd dumped my cell in the heat of inspiration. It was Hunter calling. Again.

Sighing, I told the thing to ignore the call and fell face-down onto the bed. It was obvious I couldn't keep my eyes open any longer. As much as I didn't want to interrupt the glorious gush of inspiration, falling asleep again at the writing desk wasn't going to get me anywhere. Sleep pulled at me, and I didn't have the strength to fight anymore.

Three hours later, I woke to a head full of muse-inspired story and a buzzing I vaguely remembered dreaming about. I fumbled for my phone, swiping it on without really looking at it. "Hi," I muttered.

"Terri! I'm so glad to hear your voice. Are you all right?"

His voice sent warm shivers over my body. "Didn't Shay tell you that I'm okay?"

"Yes, of course she did, but I really needed to hear that from you." He inhaled. "And I need to apologize for the way I acted when you...when you became..."

"When I shifted."

"When you shifted."

The icy lump that had been living in my heart started to melt. "I'm sorry I scared you." I swallowed back tears. "I didn't know what else to do. You're one hard-headed male, Devereux."

"That bad, huh?"

"Let's just say you're exceptionally good at that denial thing."

He groaned. "The Bigfoot was real, right?"

"Among several other folks."

"Please don't, I'm not sure I can take all this."

It was probably a little mean, but I smiled. "You'll be all right."

"As long as I don't lose you I'll be fine."

Tears blurred my vision. "Are you sure you want to be with a socially awkward, half-girl half-collie, with writing issues?"

"I don't know."

I held my breath.

"That writing issue thing is a hard one to ignore." He made a little thinking noise. "Maybe you could let your collie half try to write the next book. I know the paw to keyboard might be an issue, but we could get her one of those stick things disabled people use to type. She could hold it in her mouth, or maybe we could strap it to her head."

"You're funny, Hunter." Warm affection filled my chest. "I like that in a man."

"So, when are you coming home?"

"The thing is, I got some great advice, and while reading one of my long-time favorite novelists, it all sunk in. I started a whole different book, in a different genre, from the beginning and it's all coming together."

There was silence for a moment. "You could write here in Ugly Creek."

"I know, Hunter, but I'm afraid I'll lose the flow of my book, and I just got my mojo back. There are a lot of distractions back there." Then it dawned on me. "And you're not supposed to be one of them. I thought you were leaving."

"I discovered I couldn't do it. I had to stay and try to convince the woman I love that I'm really not as hard-headed as she thinks."

"I'm not so sure about that."

"Maybe I could be trained?"

I laughed. "Maybe. I could see if the leprechauns have any ideas."

He let out a sound that sounded like a scream stifled by a groan.

"Easy there, Devereux. They don't usually bite."

"I have to say, you tried to tell me."

"I'll be back as soon as the word rush lets up."

"See you then. I love you, Terri."

"Love you too, Hunter."

We hung up, and I took a moment to get myself calmed down. Then it was time to get back to work.

I called room service for a pot of coffee and a sandwich assortment. No, I'm not a coffee fan, but this was an emergency. While I was waiting, I went back to the spiral bound notebook where I had spent so many hours spilling out what would either be my best book ever, or the worst thing I'd ever written. Sometimes I was sure it was one, then I'd be positive it was the other. Either way, I was obsessed with finishing.

Chapter Twenty

My cell phone said it was Wednesday morning, two days before Halloween. I was heading down the Interstate toward Ugly Creek, excited to get back to the people I love—and who love me back. Tucked carefully in my small suitcase were two spiral notebooks and an inexpensive laptop containing the new, improved first draft of my latest novel. It had come so quickly I'd had a hard time writing it down even with the weird shorthand I'd developed for myself over the years, so I'd finally gone back to Walmart for a little laptop so I could type the thing out. I couldn't wait for my agent to read the manuscript, but I wanted to clean it up first. I had emailed a copy to Hunter. I wanted to know what he thought.

It was a much improved book, I was certain of that. The plot and characters were totally different from anything I'd written before. Well, except the handful of short stories I'd written back in high school. The ones I'd proudly shown to my English teacher, Ms. Hanson. I was a good student, and teachers liked me. That day, my teacher told me I had talent, but she was ashamed of me for wasting my potential writing not just commercial fiction, but the crass, ugly genre of horror. I gave up writing for years, and when I did start writing again, I wrote the more feminine, dignified genre of women's fiction.

The manuscript I'd just completed was not feminine, not dignified, not women centered. It was bloody and violent and scary. And I had enjoyed every minute I'd spent writing it.

Okay, I admit it. I was pretty damn proud of myself. Yeah, I'd have to write the contracted manuscript, but somehow that didn't seem as daunting as it had just a few days ago.

I had worked hard and long, and I was thrilled to be going home. Well, to Aunt Ruth's house actually. I was anxious to see Shay and Ace, and I missed Rose terribly. I might not have known her long, but we were connected in some inexplicable way.

Then there was Hunter. I knew there were things we would have to work out, but for the first time ever, I believed there might just be a relationship in my future. Maybe even a husband and children.

I was afraid to hope too much though. Deep in my heart was the fear that home and family were not things I could have. Maybe I was just too different. Maybe no man would be willing to take on the craziness of a wife-collie. And the idea of babies scared me to my very soul. I groaned and forced myself to focus on the road. It looked like it might rain, and drivers seemed to take more risks in the rain than when the roads were dry.

The closer I got to Ugly Creek, the darker everything became. Ominous clouds were gathering and I knew a storm was in store for the area. I hadn't heard any thunder or seen streaks of lightning yet, but it was only a matter of time. I hoped the storm would go in a different direction, but that didn't seem to be what was happening. Oh well, it wouldn't kill me to get wet. I wasn't crazy about thunder and lightning, though. Not to mention tornadoes. They weren't the huge ones like out in the Midwest, but they were terrifying just the same.

I took an exit for gas, snacks, and to check my phone for a weather update. Twenty minutes later, I had a full tank, was munching on chips, and knew there was a seventy percent chance of rain that might include thunderstorms, and there was the possibility of severe weather later in the day.

I headed home and hoped the weather wouldn't be too bad. All those hours with my head in my own world, and the weather had been sunny and beautiful. Now that I'm finished and could take a break, it does this.

Not that a little rain was going to dampen my mood. I was pretty sure I could get my career back on track, I had a little sister to love, and Hunter had finally come over to the strange side. I was a happy girl.

There was some sort of tie-up just outside Knoxville, slowing the traffic to stop, go two feet, stop again, repeat. I turned on some classic rock and munched on a candy bar. Hopefully it wouldn't be too long before I got home. Home, yeah. It felt entirely too good thinking of Ugly Creek as home. It felt right. Maybe I should just stay there. The people were accepting of odd, and there was plenty of room for my alter-ego to run and play. Maybe Hunter and I could make our home there. The idea had me smiling.

Finally traffic cleared, and I was once again on my way. The clouds were darker now. Before long I had to turn on my lights and wipers. It wasn't raining hard, but Mother Nature was obviously gearing up for a long, wet afternoon.

I smiled at the thought of curling up somewhere with Hunter while outside the rain played relaxing melodies against the roof and windows. Awesome.

A loud clap of thunder startled me so badly I jumped and hit my knee on the steering wheel. I laughed at myself and waited for the next one.

By the time I turned off the Interstate onto the Ugly Creek road, it was raining lightly at a steady pace. My phone buzzed and I smiled when I saw Shay's name.

"I'm almost there, psychic."

"Good, your dad was here."

"What did he do?"

"Nothing, actually. He came up the front steps, and I heard the back door shut. I opened the front door, but he was already heading toward the kennel, he wandered around that for a while, then took off through the woods. I found Rose's clothes on the back porch. She used the scent of the other dogs to confuse him, didn't she?"

"Yeah, but it won't last long. I'm just about to the city limits, I'll look for her."

"Be careful, Terri. The weather woman just said they think a tornado touched down near Farragut about ten minutes ago."

"I'll be careful, and I'll let you know as soon as I know something." I clicked off the phone and headed toward the most logical place, Aunt Ruth's house. It was just as likely she'd headed toward the woods.

Hunter's car was in the driveway, and I saw him at the house, running around yelling for Rose and knocking at doors and windows. I dove out of the car and onto the front porch. I unlocked the door and rushed into the house. "It's me, little sis. Are you here?" It was obvious pretty quickly that she wasn't there.

Hunter came up beside me. "Any ideas?" he asked.

"Actually, I think I might know where she is. Wanna come?"

He grabbed me and kissed me until my bones dissolved. Then he grinned at me. "Let's go find Rose."

I somehow thought to grab my bathrobe from the kitchen, then we were on our way.

By the time we reached the little clearing I recognized from before, it was raining so hard you could shower out there. I got out and headed in the direction I'd seen Rose go the other night, and heard Hunter right behind me. I called out for her, but wondered if even her ears could pick up in this deluge.

Then a familiar collie puppy came trucking out of the foliage so fast and hard she almost knocked me down. I sat on my heels and held the dog close for a moment, then stood and put my hand on Hunter's arm. "It's okay, you can stop calling for her now. Let's go."

He looked at me, then at Rose, then back at me. Even with the dark cloud cover and the pounding rain, I could see the color drain from his face. "If you say so."

I hurried Rose to my car, put her in the backseat, and wrapped her in my robe. She was shivering, so as soon as I got in I started the car and turned the heat on full blast.

Hunter climbed in the passenger side and fastened his seatbelt with shaking hands.

"Furry runs in our family," I told him.

He groaned, leaned back in his seat, and closed his eyes. I was impressed with his lack of freaking out. Maybe there was hope for the man after all.

173

It was all but impossible driving with the rain coming down so hard, but I slowly headed back toward our neighborhood. Thankfully, the rain slacked off, and it seemed that maybe the storm was over. Then I realized. "Is the sky green?"

Hunter leaned forward so he could look up better, and Rose put her paws on the door's armrest where she could see. She barked quick and sharp, and he sucked in breath and muttered. "Oh crap."

We were at Aunt Ruth's by then, and it only took a moment for the three of us to run into the house. Hunter and I grabbed blankets, pillows, couch cushions, whatever we could find. Rose and Scrappy joined us in the hall.

Rose tugged on a blanket with her teeth, pulling it toward us. She shoved Scrappy toward the blanket then stuck her nose under the edge and scrambled trying to get under with the cat.

I pulled the material tightly around them, and a moment later, my sister was human again. She held onto Scrappy, I snuggled her against me, and Hunter held me close.

We discovered that during a tornado, the wind really did sound like a train. As it blew around us, the house shook hard. The wood creaked and groaned, and I was pretty sure I heard Rose crying.

Hunter stretched one leg out, then the other, did some kind of twisting movement, and he was on the other side of my sister. He reached a long arm around both Rose and me, and we had her locked securely between us. "It's going to be okay," he told her.

She snuggled between us, Hunter and I held hands, and we waited. The roar and pounding was terrifying, the lights went out, I heard glass breaking, and the roar got even louder. It seemed to last forever.

And then it was over.

Chapter Twenty-One

The three of us, with Rose carrying Scrappy, walked together into the living room. There was a broken window, and both Aunt Ruth's and our things were scattered around by the harsh wind that had shoved its way through the house. My arm was around Rose's shoulders, and I felt her shaking. The storm had left everything a little chilly, but I'd put my money on adrenaline, not temperature. "How about we find you some clothes?"

Even her smile was shaky. "I'd like that, but I think all my stuff is at Shay's.

I hugged her close for a moment. "Shay's smaller than me, let's see if she has something that might fit you."

She frowned. "Are you sure she won't mind?"

"Of course not, she's family."

I turned to Hunter. "Rose and I are going to steal, I mean borrow, some clothes from Shay."

His mouth twitched like he was trying to hold back a smile. "I'm going to check outside."

"Be careful."

"I will." He gave me a quick kiss, squeezed Rose's shoulder, then headed for the door.

Rose was dressing when I heard a car pulling in the driveway. I looked out to see Shay and Ace jump out of his car. It was then I realized I'd left my cell phone in my car. A person cannot be faulted for not thinking straight in the middle of a damn tornado.

Rose pulled the sweater over her head and turned toward me. "Was that really a tornado?"

I looked into her wide eyes. "We won't know for sure until the experts take a look, but it sure seemed like it was."

A shiver moved through her body and I pulled her into her arms. "I'm just glad we found you before it hit."

"Me too."

Rose was crying and I was holding her close when Shay peeked into the room. When Rose finally lifted her head, Shay handed her a box of tissues. "I'm glad you found something to wear." She put a bag on the bed. "I brought some of your stuff in case you need it."

"Thank you."

Scrappy leaped up onto the bed, and Rose scoped her up.

Shay wrapped a sweater around me. "Sweetie, you're soaked."

I looked down and cringed. "I probably got you wet, Rose."

"I'm fine, but you should go change." Rose's expression was so grownup I had to catch myself to keep from laughing.

"Yes, ma'am. Let me check on Hunter first, though." I caught her eye-roll as I turned to head out.

Hunter stood at one corner of the house, conferring with Ace. I went to him and wrapped an arm around his waist. His clothes were soaked and dripped as I held on.

He pulled me close and wrapped his long arms around me. "You're freezing, sweetheart."

"So are you."

"Me big, strong man. Me be fine."

"You big, crazy nut who needs to change clothes."

"In a minute." He leaned toward me and kissed me long and carefully. When he came up for air he held my gaze. "You're going to be the death of me, woman."

"Same to you, big man."

"I'll get some clothes from the car and change, but only if you do too." He leaned close to my ear and whispered. "Preferably in the same room."

He turned to go, but I grabbed his arm. "Why do you have clothes in your car?"

He studied the ground for a moment, then met my gaze. "Because I checked out of the B&B, but my heart wouldn't let me leave."

He slipped out of my grasp and headed toward his car. I took a moment to blink back the tears, then went for the house.

****

Within two hours after the tornado, I was pretty sure everybody in Ugly Creek had ether called, come by, or was standing on our lawn. It had been a long day and I was just about ready to crash. Rose had changed to her four-legged form, run the yard for a while, and was currently curled up with Scrappy and asleep on the porch. Warm arms wrapped around me, and I leaned back against Hunter.

"Do you think anybody would notice if I became Trixie and joined them?"

"Don't know. Think they'd notice if her human boyfriend came too?"

"Terri girl." The voice came from behind and to my right.

I went rigid as I turned to face him. A furtive glance toward the porch told me that Scrappy was alone. "Hello, Daddy."

"I know you don't want me here, but I had to make sure my girls are safe."

"We're fine." Was that tears in his eyes?

"I'd like to see Rose."

"That's up to her."

"It's okay, Terri. I want to see Daddy." Rose went to him and gave him a big hug. "There was a tornado."

Daddy closed his eyes and his knees seemed to buckle. Rose had hold of him and I moved to grab his other arm. "Daddy, are you all right?"

He took a deep breath and straightened up. "So it was a tornado?" He looked from one of us to the other, and there were definitely tears in his eyes now. "I couldn't get in touch with either of you, traffic was totally stopped on the Interstate, and I was terrified my girls would get hurt."

"We're fine," I told him. "We got back here just in time and took cover in Aunt Ruth's house."

"Terri and Hunter took care of me," Rose told him.

Daddy eyed Hunter disparagingly. Hunter moved toward him and held out his hand. "My name is Hunter Devereux, and if Terri thinks she can put up with me, I hope to soon be your son-in-law."

"You'd be my brother," Rose squealed.

Hunter grinned. "I would."

"Cool." Rose hugged him, then did a little dance of joy. "Lots of family."

Speaking of which, Shay slid quietly in beside me, with Ace close behind her. "I can't believe we never knew about her," she whispered.

"We missed out," I whispered back.

Rose looked at me with a perky little grin. It's hard not to eavesdrop when you can hear a pin drop a quarter mile away. That thought brought another, and I turned to see Daddy looking at me, a sad expression pulling at his face.

"I know I screwed everything up with both of you," he said. "I scared you, Terri. Not just a little, either. I terrified you. Becky was convinced I would hurt you and, it wasn't logical, but I was afraid somehow maybe I might. So, when she asked that I not have anything to do with you, told me that it would be better if I left, I figured she was right."

I held his gaze. "I'm your daughter and I needed you."

"I know. I let fear and insecurity get in the way of what was best for my baby. I am sorry."

He turned to Rose. "I swore I'd do better with you, but then I took a job with a lot of travel, and I just sort of fell into the easy place of letting your mom take care of you. What did I know about little girls? And I sure didn't want to scare you like I did your sister."

Rose crossed her arms and settled a serious glare on him. "You weren't around and Terri and I didn't know each other, so we each had to stumble through the shifting stuff alone."

"What she said." I gave him a glare of my own.

He held up his hands in surrender. "We'll work at training."

"Wait." I took a step toward him. "You had training?"

"Some."

Rose and I exchanged a look, and he sighed. "I'll

180

train both of you."

"When?" Rose's arms were crossed over her chest and her eyes narrowed as if she dared him to say the wrong thing.

"Soon." He sighed. "Right now, I'd better get Rose back home. Her mother's worried."

Shay stepped closer. "Could you maybe stay one more day and share our Halloween party? Rose's mother is welcome to come too."

Daddy smiled. "You're Shay, aren't you?"

"Yes, I am." She looked a bit flustered.

Daddy smiled. "I've seen pictures. Besides, you look a lot like your mother."

Wait. I hoped this wasn't going where I thought it might be. "Pictures?"

Daddy looked me in the eye. "Becky sends me family pictures a couple of times a year."

"I've seen them," Rose said. "That's how I knew what you looked like."

"You've been looking through my computer?" he asked.

She lowered her head, though she didn't look all that contrite. "I happened to see the pictures one day and the next time you let me use your computer I checked them out. And found out I have a sister."

"I'm glad," he said. "I should have insisted the two of you get to know each other." He turned to Rose. "I'm staying at the local B&B. I'll get you a room there if you want, or you can stay with your sister. One more day, then back home. Understand?"

Rose grinned so big it hurt my lips to look at her. "Thanks."

Daddy sighed. "Karen's going to kill me."

Rose gave Shay the big-eyed look. "Could I stay with you tonight?"

"Of course you can stay with us. You're family."

My heart drooped. "Rose, you can stay with me. We haven't had nearly enough time together."

Rose patted my arm. "There will be plenty of time later. Right now you and Hunter need to talk."

"You're pretty grown-up for a puppy."

She grinned. "I know."

****

Thanks to my awesome family, within ten minutes, the visitors had vanished. Hunter and I stood facing each other in Aunt Ruth's living room.

He spoke first. "I'm an idiot."

I bit back the smile and put my hand against his cheek. "Just seriously stubborn."

"No wonder you were so frustrated with me." He wrapped his arms around my waist and pulled me against him. "You were trying to tell me something crucial and I wasn't listening."

"You're listening now, that's what's important." I swallowed. "You're really okay with what I am?"

His lips tightened and he looked away. "I won't say it'll be easy."

Pain tugged at my heart. I lowered my chin so he couldn't see the tears in my eyes.

"Thing is, you are the most amazing woman I've ever met. I love you too much to walk away just because you're a much better and more successful writer than I."

"What are you talking about? I'm not."

"You are." His face lit up with pride. "I read your new manuscript, and it's fantastic. You're great."

I took a moment for his words to sink in, but when they did, I looked up into a pair of mischievous eyes. "I should bite you."

His lips tugged to one side. "Promise?"

I let out a huge, heartfelt sigh as I let my forehead fall forward to lean against his shoulder. Laughter filled my belly and chest, and it came out a little at a time, until I felt his laughter mixed with mine.

"We are one weird couple," I said.

"Us? What about the B&B owner and the leprechaun. McDuffy is a real leprechaun, right?"

I studied his face for a moment, trying to make sure he really wanted to know. "Yes, he's a for-real leprechaun."

He frowned in apparent thought. "And the woman at the courthouse. Costume or real?"

"Ugly Creek is best taken one shock at a time."

He looked a little pale. "So, that's a yes."

"Enough, Hunter. There will be plenty of time later to deal with your newfound acceptance of the paranormal. I have other ideas in mind for tonight."

A smile pulled at his wide, handsome mouth. "What sort of ideas are you thinking about?"

"Well, since we finally have some time alone." I jerked his shirt out of his pants put my hands underneath, and slid my palms up his chest. "I was thinking about making up for lost time."

He groaned. "I like the way you think, sweetheart."

His hands grasped me around the waist, and before I could blink, I was thrown over his shoulder and we were headed to my bedroom. He dumped me on my bed, followed me in, and proceeded to show me just how great a man could make a woman feel.

Chapter Twenty-Two

As the sun slowly slipped behind the mountains, werewolves howled, monsters mashed, vampires snarled, ghosts moaned. What can I say, Shay had some killer Halloween music and sound effects. It would be one out-of-this-world party.

We were gathered in Ace's big white house. Rose was on the phone with her mother, trying to smooth out rumpled emotions. Hunter and Ace were doing an incredible job of decorating both outside and inside the house. Who would have thought those two could do scary weird? Shay and I were making snacks in the big, amazing chef's kitchen that Ace rarely used. What a waste.

"Did you talk to your mom?" Shay asked.

"Yeah, but it was hard to really work things out over the phone with her on the other side of the world." I stuck my finger in the cupcake icing and tasted. Perfect!

"She admitted to being in contact with Daddy, and that she had asked him to stay away." I glanced toward the door behind which my little sister was trying to make her mom understand our connection. "If it was my child, I wouldn't let anybody keep me away."

"I'm sorry."

"Thanks." My phone vibrated and I smiled when I saw the name. "Finally."

Shay had seen the name too. "Tell her I said hi."

"I was beginning to worry," I told Diara.

"Oh, so you take precious time out of your horribly busy day to call your best friend, and you're worried because she isn't right there waiting for your call?"

There was humor in her voice, but ouch! "I'm sorry, Diara. You're right, I have seriously neglected my best friend duties. I owe you."

"Yes you do. Where are you anyway? Is that Shay's Halloween music?"

"Yep. We're having a little party. That's actually why I've been trying to call you. I was hoping you could come."

"Sorry I can't make it. I was sort of hiding out."

The hurt I heard in her voice raked at my heart. "What happened?"

"When did my ability rub off on you?"

"You don't have to be psychic to hear hurt in your best friend's voice. Now, what happened?"

"Some old thing. I tried again to warn Finley about Scott, but instead of just brushing me off, she accused me of being jealous of her life. She said I was trying to break them up because I didn't want to see her happy."

"Oh Diara! I'm so sorry. I really do wish you were here. We'd have a blast tonight."

"Except the last thing I want is to get in the way of your new romance."

"You could stay with Ace and Shay."

She laughed. "Because their romance is so much older than yours. I think I'll stay here where I can watch out for my big sister."

"I'm here if you need me."

"Oh great, Mom's calling. Remember you said that

when I show up at your house screaming and crying because my sister finally shoved me over the cliff."

"I'll be right here with a good, solid rescue rope. And cookies."

Her laugh was anemic, but it was a laugh. "That's why I love you, girlfriend."

We hung up, and I turned to watch the festivities, only to find Daddy headed across the living room toward me.

"Happy Halloween, Terri."

"You too, Daddy."

He leaned close and lowered his voice. "What's up with the woman next door?"

I shrugged. "She's mean, and probably crazy."

"You watch out for her, baby."

I searched his expression. "What aren't you telling me?"

He glanced around the room, then caught my gaze. "Have you smelled anything strange in her flowerbed?"

"No. But then she doesn't let anything get close to her precious flowers."

"I don't blame her. The other day, I came by here as canine."

"Spying on us."

"I caught the scent of decomposition."

I tried to shrug it off. "It's a flowerbed. There's no telling what she's using in that thing. Plus, the demon cat probably buries his rats there."

"Demon cat?" I could tell Daddy was fighting the smile.

"We're mortal enemies. Except when we're friends."

He shook his head. "It's nothing like that. I didn't

get a chance to check it out, but it smelled a lot like human decomp."

I stared at my father. "How the heck would you know that?"

He swallowed. "Before I married your mother, my canine worked for the FBI as a cadaver dog for several years."

"Wow." I stood staring at him until he smiled gently and pulled me into his arms.

"Just watch yourself, please."

"I'll be careful, Daddy," I promised.

****

Our friends started arriving just as the sun slid behind the trees and excitement of the holiday began to grow. Jake and Stephie came dressed as rag dolls "You two are adorable," Shay said.

"Ah, he's so cute." Ace grinned at Jake.

Morticia elbowed Gomez. "Try to act civilized, Ace."

"It's okay," Jake said. "It's what you'd expect from a man who spends so much time with dogs."

Ace growled at his friend, and we all laughed. Behind me, I felt a warm hand against my back. "Tell him, Jake," Hunter said.

Hunter, dressed in a brown suit, white shirt, and bow tie; shrugged. "I've done the others from time to time. I just happen to like eleven the best."

"Terri makes an adorable space cowgirl," Shay said, looking at my brown sleeveless dress, gun belt, and fake futuristic gun.

"I think this wig makes me look like you." I pulled at the auburn curls.

"What are you talking about? My hair is black."

Shay swung some of her knee-length, black wig over her shoulder.

"More like Stephie," Jake said, and tugged at her red yarn wig.

"Hair maybe, but Shay and Terri resemble each other without props."

"Do I look like them?"

We all turned to see Rose dressed as the most adorable kitty I'd ever seen. She wore a simple brown body suit with black and tan markings to make it look more like a cat. Her ears and nose were pink, and she'd glued on whiskers, which made the costume more real and less the sexy cat costume that older women wore.

"You absolutely look like them," Stephie said. "Especially Terri."

"If she was a cat," Shay shot me a teasing grin.

I made a face back, then turned to put on some dance music. There was pizza, chips, beer and wine and soft drinks. A few trick-or-treaters came by, but most of the candy found its way into one of us.

Most of the teenagers who volunteered for Ace came by. Costumes ran from intricate science fiction robots, familiar characters from movies and TV shows, and even an odd character I wasn't positive wasn't real; to jeans and T-shirts of a regular high school student. A few neighbors and adults who supported Ace's animal rescue efforts also dropped in.

Steve and Liza came by about ten dressed as Cleopatra and Mark Antony. I was thrilled to see the couple. They ran a computer programming and support company just outside Ugly Creek. They'd had a break-in a while back, and were still working to get everything back to normal. To see them take a little time for fun thrilled me.

The opening notes of a classic rock song sounded, and I looked up in time to see Hunter's chicken head opening. I started his way, when I heard a squeal and saw Rose all but jumping up and down. Hunter looked at me and I tipped my head in her direction. He gave a tiny nod, then went over to take her hands in his. They were so entertaining everybody stopped what they were doing to watch.

"He's so much fun!" Rose told me a little later.

My heart warmed that these two who had just come into my life, but who I loved so much, got along so well. At about nine, Daddy and Rose headed out. I finally found out where my sister lives, a small place called Soddy-Daisy, which was a little town just north of Chattanooga, Tennessee. So close, and I'd had no idea.

Rose and I hugged, then made Daddy swear he'd make sure we saw each other on a regular basis. They left, I shed a few tears, then managed to get myself together enough to go back to the fun.

It seemed things were beginning to wind down a little, when a gasp came in a wave across the room. I turned to see what was up, and gasped myself. Even in Ugly Creek this was different.

Aunt Octavia wore a pinkish-tan body suit and the biggest, longest blond wig I'd ever seen. "Lady Godiva," I murmured. "Holy incredible."

Beside me, Hunter, his mouth hanging open, shook his head in disbelief.

Aunt Octavia strode into the party. "Sorry I'm late, there were a couple of other places where I had to make an appearance."

There was an immediate push toward her, but she ignored them all to head right to Stephie. A quick look at her hand, and the older woman smiled. "All is well. Happiness will increase in late spring."

Aunt Octavia turned and headed right for us. She held out her hand, and Hunter put his, palm up, in it. "Now that you removed your head from where you'd stuck it, you'll find life is much more interesting." She winked at me.

She turned to the mob of party-goers who were waiting for a reading, or to tell her how much she meant to them. She made the rounds, then joined the dancing. I was amazed by her moves, and watching her dance with a pack of young folks was possibly the most amazing thing I'd ever experienced.

Aunt Octavia was the life of the party, going strong for longer than people much younger. I have no idea what she might be, but I seriously doubt she's entirely human.

The festivities continued until after midnight. We danced, we ate junk food, and played silly games. It was a lot of fun, but Aunt Octavia left just before the witching hour, and after that people started to trickle out. We hung in until the last person left and Hunter and I helped clean up the worst before we said goodbye to Shay and Ace.

At home, Hunter locked the door behind us, and I grinned at the white and yellow ball of fur curled up on the couch. "Scrappy's worn out," I said. "Poor kitty, lying around all by herself, doing nothing."

"What about you?"

I turned to see him giving me a look that I thought might melt my panties. "What about me?"

"Are you worn out?"

"Actually," I said, as I slid off my gun belt and let it drop to the floor. "I suddenly have a lot of energy."

"Good. You're going to need it."

He was right.

I did.

A word about the author...

Cheryel Hutton is a Southern girl to the core. She was born in Tennessee, and has spent most of her life there. There among the hills and valleys she found abundant inspiration for the stories she writes.

Recently she and her husband moved near Jacksonville, Florida, where they enjoy the sunshine, warm weather, and nearness to the ocean. Here Cheryel is discovering new inspiration, and spends her time transcribing stories told to her by a muse who happens to be a dragon.

Her books include *Blood of the Innocent, Keepers of Legend, Doggone Ugly Creek, Secrets of Ugly Creek,* and *The Ugly Truth.*

You can find out more about Cheryel here:
www.cheryelhutton.com
www.dragonwhisperer.me